... were ... but
... work for their ... the
...many.

...ny of its secret agents, flo... ...pa... ...ied
Europe to harass the enemy and ... ...nce
fighters, were captured, to... ... .

This very clandestine organization was called the Special
O...tions Executive.

... who knew of it just called it SOE.

Martin Booth was born in England and lived in Hong Kong and, for a short time, in Africa until he was twenty. Well known as a novelist and a non-fiction writer, as well as a writer of films and television documentaries, he lives in the West Country with his wife. His interests include history (especially of China), wildlife conservation and foreign travel.

Books by Martin Booth

DOCTOR ILLUMINATUS
MIDNIGHT SABOTEUR
MUSIC ON THE BAMBOO RADIO
PANTHER
PoW
WAR DOG

MIDNIGHT SABOTEUR

Martin Booth

PUFFIN

PUFFIN BOOKS

Published by the Penguin Group
Penguin Books Ltd, 80 Strand, London WC2R 0RL, England
Penguin Putnam Inc., 375 Hudson Street, New York, New York 10014, USA
Penguin Books Australia Ltd, 250 Camberwell Road, Camberwell, Victoria 3124, Australia
Penguin Books Canada Ltd, 10 Alcorn Avenue, Toronto, Ontario, Canada M4V 3B2
Penguin Books India (P) Ltd, 11 Community Centre, Panchsheel Park, New Delhi – 110 017, India
Penguin Books (NZ) Ltd, Cnr Rosedale and Airborne Roads, Albany, Auckland, New Zealand
Penguin Books (South Africa) (Pty) Ltd, 24 Sturdee Avenue, Rosebank 2196, South Africa

Penguin Books Ltd, Registered Offices: 80 Strand, London WC2R 0RL, England

www.penguin.com

First published 2004
1

Copyright © Martin Booth, 2004
All rights reserved

The moral right of the author has been asserted

Set in 11¾/14¼ pt Monotype Bembo
Typeset by Rowland Phototypesetting Ltd, Bury St Edmunds, Suffolk
Made and printed in England by Clays Ltd, St Ives plc

British Library Cataloguing in Publication Data
A CIP catalogue record for this book is available from the British Library

ISBN 0–141–31526–1

For Nicola

The colophon in this book is of the Westland
Lysander aircraft, the chosen aircraft used by the SOE.
It was affectionately known as the Lizzie
by all who flew in it.

A glossary of military and other terms, and foreign
words used in the book, can be found at the end.

1

The first thing Jacob heard, even before he opened his eyes, was the sound of the postman dismounting from his bicycle and propping it against the stone platform upon which his grandfather placed the milk churns, ready for collection by the dairy lorry at half past seven every morning, rain or shine. Next came a short bark from Fix, the farm collie, followed by the familiar creak of the farmyard gate hinge, the postman's hob-nailed boots on the cobbles, a rustling as he sorted through the mail in the leather bag hanging over his shoulder then, finally, his voice.

'Plymouth were hit hard again last night,' he reported. 'The docks and naval dockyard got it bad, they did. Sky were lit up like I don't know what!' There was a customary pause as he checked the letters in his hand, ostensibly to ensure he was not delivering the wrong mail, but actually so he could nosily scrutinize it. 'Two today, Mrs Shawcross. One from London an' t'other from . . .' his voice rose half an octave to emphasize its importance and rareness '. . . India.'

Jacob swung himself over the edge of the bed and,

quickly shrugging on his clothes and hastily brushing his hair, went downstairs to find his grandmother sitting in the parlour, shelling peas into an enamel bowl. They rattled like marbles as they hit the metal. The warm sunlight of a fine summer's morning shone in through the door to the farmyard. Outside, a cockerel in its best gaudy plumage was scratching about in the earth, surrounded by a gaggle of hens.

'Morning, Gran!' Jacob greeted her.

'Well, there's nothing like the postman to get you to shake your leg!' she exclaimed, kissing him on the forehead and handing him a blue envelope. 'Here's your daddy's letter.'

Whenever a letter arrived for him, Jacob chose to sit alone on the top of the farmyard wall to read it. From his seat, he had a view of the lane all the way from the village of Oakstone to the gate leading into Shawcross Spinney, the little wood planted by his great-great-grandfather. He never opened the letter straight away but always looked at it first, turning it over, reading the postmark, trying to visualize its journey through a world at war to the safety of his hands.

The envelope had a four *anna* postage stamp in the top right-hand corner showing King George VI's head wearing a crown. The postmark was so badly smudged as to be illegible. On the reverse, the flap was overprinted with a vermilion rubber stamp: Jacob knew the letter would have been opened by the military censor to ensure it contained no information of use to the enemy. Below it was written his father's name and rank: *Adams, Michael, Major.* Slipping his penknife into the envelope, Jacob slit it open, extracted the single sheet of blue-tinted airmail onion-skin notepaper, unfolded and read it.

My Dearest Jack, it went, *I hope this finds you well – and behaving. Don't go chasing Grampy's hens! You'll put them off the lay. I'm still in India. I can't tell you exactly where, as you know – just as the posters warn us, 'careless talk costs lives!' and you never know who's listening (or reading this) – but I can tell you that it is as hot as jiggery here. I've been into the jungle where I saw a tiger, but only for a few seconds before it bounded away into the undergrowth. And I've been wearing a pair of lady's nylons! How you would laugh to see your dad, an army officer, wearing stockings! But I've found that if you wear them in the jungle, the leeches can't get a grip to bite you so they fall off. Sadly, the nylons don't stop the mosquitoes, though. Well, that's all for now. Not an hour goes by when I do not think of you. Be good – I know you will – and be brave. This war will not last forever, even if it sometimes seems as if it might. Your loving Dad. PS: Tell Grampy that here, in India, cows are considered holy and can walk where they like. They can – and do – even sleep in the middle of the road and the traffic goes round them. Tell him not to let his herd get any ideas above their station.*

Refolding it, Jacob placed the letter back in the envelope, jumped down from the wall and, going to his bedroom, placed it carefully in a wooden cigar box under his bed with the others he had received.

'Jack! Jack!' It was his grandfather's voice, calling from the barn. 'Time to see to your chores.'

'Coming, Grampy!' he called back but, before leaving his room, he looked at the calendar hanging on the wall by his bed. Taking a red wax crayon from the drawer of his bedside table, Jacob circled the date – July 23,

1942 – to show that he had received a letter. As usual, he crossed out the previous day.

As he cleaned out the milking parlour, piling the straw and dung on the muck heap, scrubbing the wooden sides of the stalls with carbolic acid solution and sluicing the cobbled floor out into the yard, Jacob could not stop himself from thinking the same thought he always had upon hearing from his father. He received a letter from India at least fortnightly. It was never long, and it rarely gave any important news, but it did tell him that his father was alive and well, and it calmed his fears that something might have happened to him. He guessed his father was in training to fight the Japanese in the jungles of Burma but it was just that, nothing more than a guess. However, at least he could assume what his father was up to; where his mother was concerned, he did not have a clue.

Unlike his father, his mother never wrote to him. When she had gone away, she had told him that she would not be able to write, and he had accepted the fact, yet it still hurt him a little. His father, busy in India, still found time to write if only one side of one sheet; his mother did not.

She had left home before his father. Major Adams had not departed for India until the previous November but his mother, Barbara, had been absent since the May before that. What she was doing to help the war effort was a mystery to Jacob.

Rinsing the milking buckets out, Jacob remembered when his mother had gone away. It had been the Wednesday after his eleventh birthday. First hugging his father tightly for over a minute, she had knelt down before him, taken him in her arms and kissed his cheek. It had not been a soft, good-night-sleep-tight type of kiss but one that was hard and, it seemed to him, somehow desperate. She had then spoken quietly into his ear.

'Jacky,' she had half-whispered, 'whatever happens, don't ever forget I love you more than anything else in the world.'

'Anything?' he had replied.

Yet she had not responded. She had just stood up and, turning, picked up her suitcase and stepped into the railway carriage, closing the door behind her. He and his father did not wait for the train to pull out of the platform, but walked away as the guard's whistle blew in the distance and the locomotive started to pump gouts of black smoke towards the railway station roof. Jacob had wanted to look back for a final glimpse of his mother, a last brief wave, yet his father was making him walk too fast to do so.

A fortnight after his mother's departure, Jacob's father took him to live with his grandparents.

'It won't be forever,' his father had told him as he helped him unpack his case in what had been his mother's bedroom when she was his age. 'Just for the duration, as they say, until the war's over and things get back to normal.'

'What about school?' Jacob had enquired, hoping that that was abandoned for the duration as well.

'All fixed up,' his father had replied. 'They'll take you at the grammar school in the town three miles away and there's an old bike in the barn.'

Over the fourteen months since the Wednesday she had departed, Jacob's mother had visited him just once, arriving unannounced, at dusk, in the week before Christmas. There was a deep covering of snow on the ground. She was wearing, he recalled, exactly the same summer clothes as she had gone away in. It was as if the seven months of her absence had been nothing more than a few hours. She brought two presents with her. One was a bottle of fine French armagnac brandy for her parents; the other was a tiny lead statue of the Eiffel Tower for him.

She stayed only for the evening, leaving again just before ten o'clock when a black Humber saloon car with military number plates drove up to the farmhouse to collect her, its headlights hooded. This time, she hugged Jacob so hard and for so long that he got pins and needles in his arm. Finally, the driver touched her gently on the shoulder and said quietly, 'We must go now, Barbara. It's only thirty minutes to take-off.'

Jacob felt as if someone was wrenching at his heart, covering him in a sodden blanket of despair. His mother saw this and, putting her arm round him, raised a smile and said what she always had when, as a little boy, he had cried.

'Don't cry, Jacky. Remember, tears don't water the flowers.'

Giving her parents a quick hug and kiss each, she walked quickly to the car, leaving her footprints in the snow. Every day for a fortnight Jacob went out to look at them until, in the first week of January, there was a sudden thaw and they disappeared as thoroughly as she had. He had heard nothing of her since then.

At noon, his milking parlour chores over, Jacob filled the water troughs from the well, emptied a bucket of slops into the pigsty and collected the eggs from the hen coop. He took them into the farmhouse just in time to see his grandmother put out the midday meal. As he was washing his hands, the water in the enamel basin grimy from his morning's work, his grandfather came in.

'Shift along there, young Jacko,' he said, grinning. 'You're not the only worker as has his hands mussed by the farmin' life.' He dipped his hands in the water and started working the coarse soap in between his fingers. 'And how many eggs did we get today, then?'

'Eight,' Jacob replied.

'Well now, from ten feathered ladies, that's not half bad, I'd say.'

They sat down side by side at the table. There was a hunk of bread, three slices of cold roast lamb, two pickled onions, an apple and a glass of cider each. A block of butter stood on a square crystal glass dish in the centre of the table.

'That butter's fresh this morning,' Jacob's grand-mother announced. 'I've done four pounds but —' she winked at her grandson '— we won't tell, will we? With food rationing, there's folk as need a bit of extra. Like old Mrs Critchley or Mrs Wallace with her two boys — and the youngest so sickly, too.'

'A pat of butter, a dozen eggs, a few extra pints of milk . . .' his grandfather said, 'they make a deal of differ-ence. Now,' he added, tossing the last crust of his bread to Fix as he did every day, the dog standing in the door-way waiting for just this ritual, 'finish your victuals and get you out to the coop. They hens need fresh beddin' in the nest boxes. Then they pigs need muckin' out and the firewood needs stackin' . . . You've a busy afternoon ahead of you, and no mistake.' He picked up his glass of cider. 'Drink up, Jacko – put some hairs on your chest.'

Jacob decided the first task he would tackle was the hen house. Stepping into its cool interior, he was struck by the smell of dank straw, feathers and the dust of dried chicken dung. It tickled his nostrils and made his mouth taste dry and gritty. As he emptied the nest boxes, the hens clucked indignantly at him, fluttering out of the door and down the ramp into their run. Several of them were followed by broods of cheeping, downy yellow chicks. Here and there, bright sunlight shone through cracks in the wooden planks of the wall, sharp pinpricks of light striking the earthen floor like the concentrated spot from a magnifying glass.

He had been working for about an hour when he heard the sound of a motorcycle. At first Jacob gave it no thought but gradually he realized it was approaching up the lane and could, therefore, only be coming to the farm, for beyond the buildings there was nothing but the spinney. Balancing on one of the ranks of nest boxes, he peeped out through the skylight in the hen-house roof just in time to see a military dispatch rider on a khaki Norton turn into the farmyard. The rider swerved round, one foot on the ground, drew to a halt and, not bothering to switch off the engine, fumbled in a canvas pannier strapped to the seat behind him. At that moment, Jacob's grandmother appeared, wiping her hands on her apron. The dispatch rider handed her something then, kicking the gear lever down and twisting the throttle, he drove out of the yard and sped back down the lane. Jacob watched him go, his head zipping along above the hedgerows.

Another hour passed. Jacob finished in the hen house and set about raking out the muck in the pigsty, the pigs' dung smelling sickly sweet. As he was shovelling the noxious mess into buckets to tip on to the vegetable garden to be raked out for manure, a small sports car entered the farmyard, briefly chased by Fix. A man in a Royal Air Force officer's uniform and carrying an official-looking briefcase got out to be met by Jacob's grandfather who, shaking the officer's hand, ushered him into the farmhouse, closing the door behind them.

Jacob waited a moment before walking over to admire the car. It was an open, pillarbox red, two-seater Singer Nine with matching red leather seats and inner door panels. The steering wheel and gearstick knob were made of highly varnished wood and the chromium plating of the radiator, headlights and hub bosses gleamed. The wheel spokes were painted silver and even the tyres looked as if they had been buffed up with shoe polish, except where the dust of the lane was sticking to them. He would have loved a ride in it but he didn't feel he could ask for one. Besides, he had to complete his farm work.

The officer stayed only a short while and was gone in fifteen minutes, placing his briefcase on the passenger seat before starting the engine and reversing carefully out into the lane.

By four o'clock, all his chores done, Jacob returned to the farmhouse for tea but, the moment he entered the kitchen, he sensed something was wrong. The kettle was not on the hearth and the tea things were not on the table. Indeed, the fire in the cooking range had almost gone out. Knowing it had to be kept in at all times, he set about adding kindling wood to the glowing embers, blowing to get them alight. It was some minutes before he could add a few logs and be sure they would catch.

As he stood up, his grandmother came into the kitchen. He noticed her eyes were red, as if she had been rubbing them, and her cheeks were sallow. She looked, he thought, suddenly very old. Behind her came his grandfather. Without saying anything, she filled the kettle from a jug and placed it on the hot plate.

'Who was the man on the motorbike?' Jacob asked.

'Telegram rider,' his grandfather replied abruptly.

'And who was the man in the car?'

His grandfather hesitated for a moment then answered, 'Just an officer friend from the aerodrome over Oakstone way.' He put his hand on Jacob's arm. 'I need to stay here with your grandma a mite longer. Think you can bring in they cows for milkin'?'

Jacob had often watched his grandfather call the cows in, yet he had never done it himself.

'I'll try,' he replied, proud to have been entrusted with this job for the first time.

'Fix'll lend you a paw,' his grandfather said.

It was not as difficult as Jacob had expected. As he opened the gate to the meadow, he whistled as his grand-father did. The cattle all looked up in their idle, bovine fashion and began to meander slowly towards him across the grass. Fix ran round the edge of the small herd to chivvy it along but the cows ignored him. They knew the routine and would not be rushed. Reaching the gate, they ambled through in single file, chewing the cud and splattering dung on the dusty earth, their ears flicking away pestering flies. At the farmyard, they strolled past the haystacks, turned left round the end of the barn and wandered into the milking parlour, their heavy udders swaying between their hind legs like grotesque sets of pink bagpipes. Following them in, Jacob found each of them in a milking stall, standing patiently waiting to be milked.

Usually his grandparents milked the cows together. However, when the parlour door opened, only his grandfather appeared.

'Gran's busy,' he announced, 'so it's you 'n' me's goin' to see to the ladies. You remember how 'tis done?'

Jacob nodded and, taking one of the three-legged milking stools, positioned himself at the rear end of the nearest cow, a honey-coloured Guernsey. Putting a wooden pail in place and reaching beneath its hind-quarters, he put his fingers round two of the cow's teats. They were warm and soft. Gently squeezing and pulling downwards, the first jets of milk squirted out to splash into the pail.

It took Jacob and his grandfather over an hour to milk the sixteen cows in the herd. By the time they were done, and the milk was in the churns and ready for collection, the cattle back out in the meadows for the night and the parlour cleaned, it was well after seven o'clock.

All through supper Jacob's grandmother, who usually chattered away, hardly spoke at all. Jacob tried without success to get her to talk. She just sat silently across the table from him, picking at her food. His grandfather made all the conversation but even this was somehow strained and false. When they finished eating, Jacob washed the dishes as his grandmother sat by the stove with the radio on, but he could tell she was not listening to it.

'Gran's not ill, is she?' he whispered to his grandfather, who was drying the plates.

'No,' was the terse reply.

When the cutlery had been put away and the crockery was back on the dresser, Jacob left the kitchen and went into the front room. Whatever it was that had upset his grandmother, he reasoned it had to be to do with that telegram. Its delivery – and the arrival soon after of the officer – were the only things that had happened that day that were out of the ordinary.

Next to the window stood his grandparents' bureau. He opened the top and lowered it quietly. Held in place by a glass paperweight was the telegram, the message printed on a paper strip that had been stuck to the buff-coloured delivery form. It read simply:

REGRET VALERIAN
COMPROMISED – STOP

It made absolutely no sense to him.

Jacob closed the bureau and returned to the kitchen. His grandmother was sitting hunched forward, her head in her hands. His grandfather was standing at her side, his gnarled hand on her shoulder. He looked somehow bewildered and at a loss.

'What's the matter?' Jacob ventured.

His grandfather took a moment to reply. 'Nothin',
Jacko.' He attempted a smile but failed. 'Nothin'.'

'Can I do something?' Jacob offered, the tense atmos-
phere in the room unnerving him.

'Just run along for a few minutes,' his grandfather
answered. 'See Fix has his meat.'

Jacob went outside. Across the farmyard, the dog was
wolfing down a bowl of scraps. He returned to the
kitchen.

'He's got his food,' Jacob said then, unable to contain
his curiosity further, added, 'Grampy, who is Valerian?'

At the name, his grandmother looked up and stared at
him. Her cheeks were wet with tears.

Jacob felt suddenly very guilty and said, sheepishly,
'I'm sorry, Gran. I looked in your bureau.'

He expected to be told off but, instead, his grandmother reached out and took his hand. She pulled him
close, kissed him, then looked up at her husband.

'Valerian's your mother,' he said bluntly.

This confused Jacob all the more. His mother's name
was Barbara. Her friends called her Babs. If she was
Valerian, he thought, they would surely call her Val.
Besides, he thought, Valerian was a man's name. He was
certain there had been a Roman emperor or general
called Valerian. Nevertheless, he decided to let this go
for the moment.

'What does *compromised* mean?' he went on.

His grandmother forced back a sob while his grandfather lowered himself heavily into the old rocking chair
at the other side of the stove from his wife.

'Sit down, Jacob,' he said. 'You're soon to be a man,
and I dare say 'tis time you knew how things are.'

Jacob sat on a chair at the table. His grandmother put her hand on his where it rested on his knee. Her fingers were warm and soft and dry.

'You know your mum's away to the war,' his grandfather began, 'but not like your dad, in a uniform. She's what they call an agent. Now, you know how 'tis presently in France?'

'France is occupied by the Nazis,' Jacob replied.

'Indeed 'tis,' his grandfather confirmed, 'but that doesn't mean we're doin' nothin' over there. These agents're in France.'

'How do they get there?' Jacob wanted to know.

'They are flown in secretly, at night. Some go in by parachute. Once there, 'tis their job to cause trouble for the enemy.'

'Cause trouble?' Jacob repeated. 'What kind of trouble?'

'You don't just fight a war with bullets and bombs,' his grandfather explained. 'There's what they call sabotage, too: blowin' up railway tracks or bridges with dynamite, smashin' up factories or power stations, cuttin' telephone lines or electricity cables. Some help patriotic Frenchmen fightin' the Germans or send back information – military intelligence, they call it – that tells us what they Germans is up to. These Frenchmen call themselves the Resistance. Mind you,' he went on, 'not all they Frenchies is good uns. There's some has turned traitor and have sided with the Nazis. They call them Quislings.'

'And my mother?' Jacob asked.

'In France.'

'Why did she have to go to France?'

'Before she met your dad and you were born,' his grandfather continued, 'your mother worked for several years in France. She were a dancer, in the theatre. After she were married, your dad and her used to go on their holidays to France.' A faraway look came momentarily to his face. 'My! They did love it there! So stands to reason she speaks French like a Frenchman. The military authorities wanted people as knows the lingo. She didn't have to go. She volunteered. Wanted to do her bit.'

For a long moment, Jacob tried without much success to imagine his mother climbing a French telegraph pole in the middle of the night with a pair of wire-cutters in her teeth. To envisage her blowing up a railway line was more than he could even attempt to visualize.

'You mustn't talk about this,' his grandfather added. ''Tis secret, as secret as secret can be. Even British folk don't know of it. So you must keep it to yourself. You won't let that slip your mind, will you?'

'No,' Jacob said, 'but why's she changed her name?'

'She hasn't,' his grandfather retorted. 'Agents don't use their real names, but what they call a code name. Your mum's is Valerian.'

Jacob was silent for a minute then, finally, he asked, 'What does *compromised* mean?'

His grandmother, her voice so low as to be barely heard, said, 'It means the Nazis have caught her.'

As the enormity of this dawned on him, Jacob felt a coldness grip his heart, spreading out through his body as if his blood were turning to ice. An awful, abiding terror began to overpower him. His stomach turned, as if he were about to vomit.

'What will happen, Grampy?' he said, immediately fearful of the reply.

Jacob's grandmother's hand tightened on his. A new trickle of tears began to run down her cheeks, dripping off her chin on to her blouse, leaving dark stains on the blue material.

At first his grandfather made no answer. He stared at the stove, the flames flickering dull orange behind the mica window in the fire door. When he spoke, his words seemed to be catching in his throat. 'In war,' he murmured, as much to himself as to Jacob, 'these things do come to pass and there ain't a damn thing we can do except pray.'

That night Jacob could not get to sleep. It was not just that he was deeply worried but he was also angry, with the war and with himself. He wanted to do something, not just lie there, tossing and turning and fretting. Yet quite what he could do other than pray was beyond him and his uselessness made him all the more frustrated.

Not long after midnight, he got out of bed and sat in his bedroom window. It was a still night, with a new moon setting over Shawcross Spinney. Somewhere in the trees a tawny owl was calling, the sound eerie in the calm night air. At the far end of the farmyard something was rooting about in the haystack. Jacob concentrated on it trying, if only for a moment, to let the distraction drive his other thoughts away. Yet it was no good: in a matter of seconds, he could tell from the way it shuffled when it moved that the creature was a badger. His worries crowded back into his mind like a dark, impenetrable fog.

As he watched it, the badger suddenly halted, briefly

sniffed the air and scuttled off hurriedly. Something had scared it. Jacob scanned the farmyard, his eyes accustomed to the different shades of darkness. It could not have been Fix: he was chained to his kennel. If it were a fox or a man coming to steal eggs – as had happened once before – the dog would have raised the alarm.

Gradually the night air seemed to fill with a distant, almost imperceptible purr that, second by second, grew in volume to become a monotonous, rhythmical throb. Jacob knew what was coming. It regularly happened whenever the weather was fair. He watched the sky above the spinney.

In a few moments a dark shape appeared, moving across the backdrop of the night. In the moonlight, he could easily make out its silhouette. It was a single-engined aircraft with high mounted wings. Its tail fin somehow looked too large and out of proportion to the rest of the fuselage, and its wheels were housed in distinctive bulging nacelles. It was gaining altitude slowly, banking to one side as it crossed in front of the moon. The light struck off the wings and through the long perspex canopy of the cockpit, as if signalling a brief farewell message to those left behind.

The sonorous, almost ponderous drone alone was enough for Jacob to identify the aircraft. It was not the deep thunder of an Avro Lancaster bomber or the urgent staccato roar of a Spitfire. Besides, when out snaring rabbits with his grandfather along the hedgerows, he had seen this aircraft from time to time parked up on the grass apron before its camouflaged hangar at the nearby airfield. This was a Westland Lysander.

2

By ten o'clock the following morning, the cleaning of the milking parlour completed, Jacob was sitting on the edge of the row of nest boxes in the semi-darkness of the hen house, the egg-collecting bucket at his feet, attempting to put his thoughts in order. He knew he had to face the situation logically, like one of the algebraic equations he had struggled with in school the previous term. As his mathematics teacher, Mr 'Stodgy' Stodgell, was forever drumming into the class, there was always an answer to be had in maths, for maths was based on reason: it was just a matter of, 'AFT, boys! AFT!' *Assessing the components, Finding the common denominator and Teasing the answer out.* The trouble was that the solution to this equation was not based upon the rational structure of mathematics and seemed truly impossible to work out.

To get things straight, Jacob cast his mind back to the last time he had seen his mother. He tried hard to recall her conversation, in the hope that she might have mentioned at least a clue as to where in France she was living, but he could remember nothing that was said. She could, he considered, be staying in Paris, for she had brought him the model of the Eiffel Tower, yet no sooner had this possibility dawned on him than he dismissed it. It was inconclusive and proved nothing: she could have purchased it anywhere. Thinking through her visit, Jacob did however recollect one piece of conversation, just before she left. It was what the driver of the car had said: *We must go now. It's only thirty minutes to take-off.*

That his mother had flown to and from France he accepted as fact. His grandfather had said agents were flown or parachuted into enemy territory and it was the logical way to get her there. Now, he pondered, if she was to have taken off within thirty minutes of being at the farm, wherever she flew from had not to be far away. This realization had no sooner dawned on him than Jacob knew the answer: his mother must have departed from the nearby Oakstone airfield.

He slid off the nest boxes and started to collect the new-laid eggs.

The airfield was a small RAF establishment with a grass runway less than half a mile long, one of scores dotted about the British countryside to confuse enemy bombers. From time to time Jacob had seen Spitfires, and on one occasion a Typhoon, land there but the only aircraft permanently on station were two cumbersome-looking Lysanders.

Pushing his hand under the belly feathers of an obstinate hen that stubbornly refused to move off its nest, he felt for the egg it was sitting on. The straw beneath the bird was warm, the new-laid egg dry and smooth when his fingers found and closed round it. Close to his face was the hen's head, its beak uttering a faint croak of annoyance and its beady eye staring at him, its skinny eyelid blinking.

Jacob stood up, narrowly missing cracking his forehead on a beam in the roof, the egg secure in his hand. Suddenly, the equation was solved. What was it, he thought, Stodgy declared whenever he completed a calculation on the blackboard? Then he remembered.

'QED!' Jacob exclaimed. '*Quod erat demonstrandum!* That's Latin for "That proves it",' he explained to the hen.

The bird, alarmed at this outburst, scuttled off its nest and out into the sunlight.

All the eggs collected, Jacob went to his bedroom and sat at the window looking down on the farmyard. Fix lay on his side in the sun, asleep. His paws twitched in a canine dream of rounding up cows or chasing hares. A few hens scratched about in the earth. From the direction of the pigsty came a deep-throated grunt followed by a piglet's brief squeal. There was such an enduring peacefulness about the scene, it was hard to imagine the world was embroiled in a desperate war.

Sitting there, Jacob felt a strange resolve mingled with a terrible apprehension. His mother's life was in danger and his father was thousands of miles away in India. It was, he considered, up to him to accept responsibility and act. At the same time he knew that what he was thinking of doing was dangerous. Very dangerous. Indeed, if it was at all possible . . .

When he went down at midday for a meal of bread, cheese and pickles, Jacob could see his grandmother had been crying again. His grandfather sat at the table with shoulders hunched, as if a huge invisible weight was relentlessly pressing down on him. Throughout the meal, little was spoken. Even Fix, waiting optimistically for his crust at the door, seemed dejected.

'Is there anything you want me to do this afternoon, Grampy?' Jacob offered as his grandmother screwed the top on the pickle jar and put the cheese away in the pantry.

'No,' came the abrupt response, as his grandfather slammed the cork in the stone cider flagon with the flat of his hand. 'Least, not till milkin'.'

After helping to clear the table, Jacob left the farmhouse and set off across the fields. The dairy cattle in the cow pasture followed him out of bovine inquisitiveness, while Fix tagged along in case there was work to do. Reaching the stile into Shawcross Spinney, Jacob sent the dog back and climbed over into the wood. It was cool in the shade of the oaks and beeches, and the ground was soft underfoot. At the far side of the spinney Jacob halted and looked ahead. There were two meadows between him and the perimeter of the airfield. The grass in them was long, almost ready for the hay cutter, and glistening with the bright gold of buttercups mingled with the scarlet of field poppies. It would, he was certain, give him enough cover to creep up to the edge of the airfield but he chose instead to walk openly across the fields and through the gate in the thick hedge that separated them. It was, he considered, better not to arouse suspicion.

Along the boundary of the airfield was a ditch then a fence of posts strung with three strands of barbed wire. Beyond, the grass was cut as short as a cricket pitch with white daisies growing out of it in clumps. Across the far side of the airfield was a small wood just inside of which stood two hangars and half a dozen arched Nissen huts, camouflage netting draped over them. In front of one of the hangars stood a Lysander.

Jacob jumped the ditch and, stretching two of the barbed-wire strands apart, eased himself between them and set off across the grass, keeping an eye out in case there was an aircraft coming in to land. He was halfway to the hangars before anyone spied him.

'Oi! You!' a voice shouted.

Jacob turned. An airman was jogging across the grass towards him, a .303 rifle slung over his shoulder, his gas-mask bag banging against his hip.

'What d'you think you're doing?' the airman continued as he came up to him. Upon his arm were sewn the three stripes of a flight sergeant. 'Don't you know this area's restricted?'

'I live in Shawcross Farm,' Jacob replied, trying to sound as innocent as possible and pointing in the direction he had come. 'My grandfather's Mr Shawcross. My name's Jacob. I,' he paused for effect, 'wanted to see the Lysander.'

'You wanted to see the Lysander!' the flight sergeant echoed incredulously. 'Don't you know there's a war on?' He then softened. 'So you know it's a Lizzie. You like aircraft, do you, son?'

'I'd like to be a pilot when I grow up,' Jacob announced although, until that minute, the thought had never entered his head.

Grinning, the flight sergeant squatted down, his head on a level with Jacob's, and looked him straight in the eye. 'You're not a Nazi spy, are you, son?'

'No,' Jacob said emphatically, shaking his head vigorously.

'In that case, I see no harm in it. But don't you go telling all your pals at school. We don't do guided tours.'

Jacob followed the flight sergeant across to the hangar. The aircraft stood on a patch of bare earth in front of the hangar, the soil patchy with spilt oil. Above it, suspended from the surrounding trees, was the camouflage net hung with strips of green and brown cloth. To one side was a stack of wooden crates, khaki-painted ammunition boxes and oil drums marked *Aviation Fuel*.

'There she is, Jacob,' the flight sergeant said with more than a passing sense of pride. 'Lizzie, the Westland Lysander.'

Close up, Jacob could see the aircraft was mostly made not of metal, as he had expected, but of a sort of cloth.

'What is this made of?' he enquired, touching the fuselage.

'It should be aluminium. That's the metal usually used in making aircraft because it's not heavy – and aircraft have to be as light as possible. But aluminium is scarce in wartime,' the flight sergeant answered him. 'So instead of ally, the airframe is made of wood and tightly covered with canvas which is then painted with a liquid called dope. When it dries, this makes it even tighter still and very strong.' He drummed his finger on the aircraft to prove his point.

'So it's really a canvas Lizzie,' Jacob replied.

The flight sergeant laughed and said, 'Yes, I suppose it is. But the sides of the cockpit and the engine are encased in aluminium. And the wings are made of metal.'

Jacob looked up. Each wing had strangely angled leading and trailing edges and seemed to tilt upwards slightly, supported by a Y-shaped strut. They joined in the centre of the aircraft above and just behind the cockpit. The wheels were fixed and unable to retract into the fuselage. Unlike any other aircraft Jacob had seen, it was painted entirely in matt black with not even an RAF roundel or recognition letters on it.

'She's got a nine-cylinder engine,' the flight sergeant continued, pointing to the nose of the aircraft where an inspection panel had been removed, showing an intricate tangle of copper pipes, wires and steel casings. The boss of the three-bladed propeller had also been removed and lay on a tarpaulin on the ground. 'She has a top speed of 212 miles an hour and she can go 600 miles without refuelling. Her ceiling is 21,000 feet – that means the maximum altitude at which she can fly. This version carries one pilot and two passengers. Or,' he grinned, 'four at a pinch with no luggage.'

'That's not much,' Jacob declared. 'A Spitfire can fly to 36,000 feet at 370 miles an hour and has a range of 1100 miles.'

'You do know your aeroplanes!' the flight sergeant retorted. 'But it's horses for courses. A Spitfire's a fighter and Lizzie is a . . . Well, let's say she has a different job.' He patted the aircraft much as one might a favourite pony. 'But Lizzie can do something a Spitfire can't.' He did not wait for Jacob to enquire what it was. 'She can take off in less than three football pitches of rough, unprepared ground. A cow meadow, a field of wheat. You name it, she'll take it. Tough as a tank she is.'

'Where are the guns?' Jacob asked.

The flight sergeant pointed to the wheels. 'In the fairing. That's the wheel casing. One Browning machine gun in each. Would you like to see inside the cockpit?'

Jacob nodded. This was far more than he had expected. All he thought he would have achieved was a quick look round before someone collared him and saw him off the airfield with a flea in his ear.

'You hold on to me,' the flight sergeant instructed. 'Now, one foot goes in that hole in the wheel fairing, the next on this little triangular plate here, the next in this hole here and up.'

It was not at all easy. The steps were far apart but the flight sergeant pushed Jacob up and he was soon straddling the side of the cockpit. The perspex canopy was open, vaguely reminding Jacob of a small elongated greenhouse. Before him was the pilot's seat, the joystick and the arched instrument panel. Once the pilot was in, Jacob thought, it must be very cramped. The flight sergeant held Jacob steady and, leaning over his shoulder, pointed to the various instruments and equipment.

'That's the altimeter, the artificial horizon, the fuel gauge, the compass . . .' He listed them one by one. 'The red, blue and white levers are the throttle controls. This panel is the radio.'

To one side hung a flexible rubber tube, stiffened with wire rings.

'What's this for?' Jacob asked.

'That's where the pilot plugs into the oxygen supply if he is flying at the ceiling altitude. There's not a lot of air up that high.'

Behind the pilot's seat, between it and the rear section

25

of the cockpit, was a huge, grey metal tank held in place by the airframe attached to the wings.

'What's that?' Jacob asked.

'That's the fuel tank,' the flight sergeant replied, adding soberly, 'If you get hit there, your next stop'll be the Pearly Gates and a set of angel's wings.'

'How does the pilot get in the back?'

The flight sergeant lifted Jacob down and they walked round to the left-hand side of the Lysander. As they went, Jacob saw his plan dissolving. There was no way he could get into this aircraft unaided. Yet, as they ducked under the port wing, his spirits soared. There was a small ladder attached to the side of the fuselage.

'Up you go!' the flight sergeant said and, as Jacob climbed the ladder, went on, 'Once airborne, the pilot can't come back here. The passengers can only contact him through the intercom.'

The rear canopy was also open. Jacob studied the cabin. It contained two small, rear-facing seats and little else. With just one person aboard, it would be confined; with two, it would be like playing sardines. However, he noticed that to the rear of the cabin, the bulkhead did not reach the floor.

'Can I get in?' he asked.

'Be careful,' the flight sergeant warned. 'If you break anything, you'll slow up the war effort.'

Jacob climbed into the rear cabin, eased himself down on to one of the narrow seats then sat on it. Being inside the aircraft, he was now out of the flight sergeant's view. Kneeling on the floor, he bent down and looked through the gap in the base of the rear bulkhead. There was a space behind it, large enough for a small amount of baggage or equipment. He stood up and peered over the rim of the canopy.

'It's not very big in here,' he remarked.

'No,' the flight sergeant replied, 'it's not first class accommodation.'

'Why is it painted black?' Jacob asked as he lowered himself to the ground. 'Spitfires are painted brown and green camouflage with light grey undersides.'

'I can't tell you that,' the flight sergeant answered.

Yet Jacob knew. It was black because it only flew on night operations.

An aircraftsman came out of the hangar, carrying a box of tools in one hand and a jerry can of oil in the other.

'Who's this then, sarge?'

'This is Jacob. Wants to be a pilot.'

The aircraftsman raised his eyebrows and exclaimed, 'Naw! Yer don't wanna do that. All that dodgin' and weavin' and divin' and bumpin' about. Turns yer tummy right over. Take a bit of advice, sunny Jim. Keep your toes on the turf.' He turned to the flight sergeant. 'Got a bit of a problem with the variable pitch gear,' he said.

The flight sergeant looked at his watch and replied, 'Well, Archie, you've got five hours to get it ironed out. This one's on a sortie tonight.'

The buckles on Jacob's school satchel would only close on the last hole. He was not surprised. Inside it he had crammed two shirts, a pullover, three vests, two pairs of socks and underpants, three handkerchiefs, a pair of corduroy trousers and a belt. In the outside pocket, he had managed to fit a large pre-war AA roadmap book of France which he discovered on the bookcase in the sitting room and which his parents had used on their motoring holidays. Next to it he slid in his father's leather-cased silver hip flask filled with water – which, although Jacob had flushed it out half a dozen times, still tasted distinctly of whisky – a penknife with a horn handle, a roll of bandage, two safety pins and six aspirin tablets.

Jacob glanced out of his bedroom window. The sun had set and the twilight was deepening. It was time to move. Hiding the satchel under his bed, he went downstairs to where his grandparents were sitting in the kitchen listening to the radio by the light of the stove. As he reached the doorway, he heard the BBC announcer: *Here is the nine o'clock news and this is Alvar Liddell reading it – RAF Bomber Command has launched its second thousand-bomber raid against Germany in three days. The target was the industrial city of Essen in the Ruhr . . .* Knowing not to speak during the headlines, Jacob stood by his grandmother's side until his grandfather switched the radio off.

'I came down to say goodnight,' he said as the light faded behind the dial of the radio.

His grandmother kissed him, and his grandfather tousled his hair and said, 'Goodnight, Jacko. Sleep tight and try not to worry.'

'Don't you worry either, Grampy,' Jacob replied then, giving Fix a stroke, he poured himself a glass of milk from a jug in the pantry, went back upstairs and closed his bedroom door.

Stripping to the waist, he hastily put on two clean vests, a thick cotton shirt, a sleeveless jumper and a heavy woollen pullover, taking care that all the clothing was a dark colour. He then rolled two pairs of long football socks on to his feet and tugged on his black school shoes. Satisfied that he could still move, he glanced at himself in the mirror, his reflection bringing a wry smile to his face. From the waist down, he looked comparatively normal – black shoes and brown corduroy trousers – but from the belt up he seemed to swell out.

It was time.

Deftly tearing a page from the middle of an exercise book, he took great care not to bend the staples out of shape. With German submarines attacking merchant ships coming to Britain, there was a paper shortage and, he considered, if one of the teachers discovered he had defaced his book there would be hell to pay. Yet no sooner had the thought occurred to him than he realized it might not matter. He might not come back – and the fate he would face would be far worse than a hundred lines or detention on Wednesday afternoon.

Resting on his chest of drawers, Jacob unscrewed his fountain pen, shook it to get the ink flowing and wrote, *Dear Gran & Grampy, I have gone to see what I can do to rescue Mum. I shall be quite safe very carefull and will be back as soon as possible. Lots of love, Jacob.* Having read the note through and correcting his spelling of *careful*, he folded the paper over to make a little tent of it and propped it on his pillow. It was strange, he thought: by the time his grandparents read the note, he would, if luck was on his side, be in occupied France. If it was against him, he would be back in bed by midnight and they would be none the wiser.

Swallowing back the glass of milk, Jacob clutched his satchel and, slowly opening his bedroom door, descended the stairs on tiptoe. The radio had been switched back on, the music programme drowning the creaking of the wooden steps. The kitchen door was ajar, a vague shimmer of warm light drifting over the floor from the stove fire door. Through the crack, he could see his grandparents as he had left them, sitting either side of the stove and lost in their thoughts. Fix was asleep on the flagstones between them. The only other light was that from the radio dial. He was, for just a moment, tempted to stay. When they found his note they would be distraught, he knew, his actions an added burden of worry. Yet, thrusting these thoughts aside, he turned and, tiptoeing out into the farmyard, headed for the fields, not looking back.

Although it was nearly dark, there was still sufficient light in the sky for Jacob to follow his footsteps from the afternoon in the long grass. Arriving at the ditch, he crouched down and surveyed the perimeter fence of the airfield. There seemed to be no sentries on duty. In the hangar, several lamps were switched on but they were hooded and contained low wattage bulbs, casting only faint circles of light. No lights shone from the Nissen huts. The windows, he considered, had almost certainly been covered with blackout curtains. The outline of the Lysander showed it had not been moved since earlier in the day.

Pushing his satchel ahead of him, Jacob squeezed under the lowest strand of barbed wire and started to crawl across the short airfield grass. With every metre, his heart raced faster.

He was halfway to the aircraft when he saw three men standing in the hangar. One was dressed in a trilby hat and gabardine raincoat and held a briefcase; the second was in a pilot's flying suit; the third he recognized as the flight sergeant. Diverting to one side, Jacob headed for the cover of the ammunition boxes and barrels of aviation fuel. He had just made the safety of their shadows when the trio left the hangar and walked towards the aircraft. As they drew nearer he could hear them speaking.

'You've a good night for it, sir,' the flight sergeant remarked.

'Yes, Flight Sergeant,' the pilot replied, slipping a flight plan map into the transparent pocket on the leg of his flying suit. 'Just enough moonlight to see by but not be seen. Light winds over the Channel. Flying time should be about ninety minutes. If there are no hitches.'

Jacob studied the aircraft. The canopy over both sections was open. A fuel line ran from a hand pump in one of the barrels to the aircraft.

'It makes me very sad to think, Wing Commander,' the third man said with a pronounced French accent, 'that you will be in *la belle France* so soon. But I? I will remain here, so near yet so far.'

The men reached the plane, disappearing from Jacob's view round the far side of it. Their voices became muffled.

Slipping out from behind the barrels, Jacob edged cautiously towards the Lysander, taking care not to step on anything that might make a sound and give him away. Yet he had no need for concern for the ground was swept clean. He reached the ladder into the rear compartment. His heart beat fast, his hands clammy, his forehead breaking into a sweat, his scalp itchy. Until now, it had all been just a plan. For a brief moment he paused. He had never even been in an aircraft before, that afternoon excepted.

A wave of panic and fear spread over him. In addition to his flying suit, the pilot was also wearing a fleece-lined flying jacket and a leather flying helmet; and he had a parachute. Jacob had on only two vests, a shirt and two pullovers. If they flew high, he knew the pilot could switch on to a tank of oxygen to breathe: he had nothing. Worse, he thought, if they met a Luftwaffe Messer-schmitt night fighter or were hit by anti-aircraft fire from the ground, the pilot had that parachute . . .

It was then, in his mind's eye, Jacob saw the telegram – *Regret Valerian compromised* – and, stretching up, put his foot on the first rung of the ladder. The aircraft swayed slightly under his weight. He paused. It settled. Slowly, he climbed higher until he reached the rim of the canopy. The men were further forward, in front of the aircraft's wing. It was dark inside the fuselage but, remembering the position of the seat and swinging his legs over, Jacob lowered himself into the compartment and on to it.

The rear section of the aircraft contained half a dozen long, thin plywood boxes bound with steel strips, two canvas kitbags, five metal boxes with heavy clasps and some tubular cardboard containers. Everything was held in place by rope netting. One of the seats had a small box marked with a red cross strapped to it; the other was vacant. For a moment, Jacob did not see the significance of this. Then it dawned on him. There was going to be a passenger.

Steps approached the aircraft. Jacob could tell they belonged to two men.

'Everything ready?' asked the flight sergeant.

'Yes, sir.' It was Archie's voice. 'Weather report in, sir.' There was a rustling of paper. 'Summer storm brewing up over the Channel Islands, sir.'

Another voice Jacob had not yet heard then spoke. 'The coded message went out over the BBC at seven. Skillet from the Mercator circuit will be waiting for you at the landing site. Give him this, will you? It contains a quarter of a million francs.'

'Certainly, sir,' replied the pilot. 'If you don't hear of me again, I'll be in Switzerland, opening a bank account.'

This remark was met by soft laughter, but Jacob could tell it was strained.

'Take care, Wing Commander.'

'*Bonne chance, mon ami.* And thank you for what you are doing for France.'

'I'll be back in five hours, sir. God willing . . .'

All the while they were talking, Jacob squeezed himself feet first through the gap under the rear bulkhead. It was a tight fit. His extra clothing had made him bulkier than he had thought. He had just got his head in when someone else climbed into the compartment and fastened the Frenchman's briefcase and a leather bag like a doctor's instrument case into the second seat, tying them in place with the seat harness. The canopy was closed and the aircraft rocked as the person climbed down and stepped off on to the ground.

33

Jacob inwardly sighed with relief. He was alone and began to ease himself out from behind the bulkhead. The thought of spending an hour and a half squeezed in behind it was not appealing.

The aircraft rocked to and fro again as the pilot climbed in. There was a pause and a lot of scrabbling noises as he settled himself into the cockpit. A series of clicks suggested he was flicking switches on. This was followed by a whining of the inertia starting motor; then, once the engine fired, the whole Lysander began to vibrate. The propeller spun faster, the noise filling the compartment increased from a shrill whine to a deep rumble.

Just as Jacob got his feet out of his former hiding place, the aircraft lurched and began to roll forwards, turning slowly. The pitch of the engine rose to a scream, the Lysander beginning to accelerate as it moved over the grass, bumping and rolling as it gathered speed.

After a hundred metres, Jacob felt the tail of the aircraft lift off the ground. Holding firmly on to the cargo netting, he stood up and gazed out the side of the canopy. In the distance, he could make out his grandfather's farmhouse, the hedges moving rapidly by.

Suddenly, the bumping ceased and the Lysander lifted smoothly into the air.

3

The Lysander gained altitude slowly, the sound of the engine changing tone as it achieved its cruising speed. Jacob, aware the pilot could not see him, gazed through the rear canopy, enraptured as the countryside moved inexorably by underneath his feet. The fields and woods made a curious jigsaw in the faint moonlight, the villages appearing as darker, irregular smudges upon the landscape. Not a single light showed anywhere other than in the blanket of stars over his head, punctuated by patches of white-tinged cloud.

Not ten minutes after taking off, the Lysander crossed the English coast, passing over an estuary and heading out across the Channel for France. The moonlight glistened on the rippling surface of the sea. Several times the plane lurched as a crosswind hit in. Far off to the right Jacob could see distant flashes that he assumed was lightning accompanying the storm about which Archie had warned the pilot.

As the shores of France came into view, the Lysander began to ascend sharply. Jacob sat down on the plywood boxes, bracing himself against the bulkhead with his feet, his hands gripping the netting once more. The aircraft bucked about violently for some minutes. Jacob rose clear of the boxes, only to slam painfully back down on them a second later. At the same time he was swung from side to side, his arms hardly strong enough to prevent him from being catapulted into the sides of the compartment. The motion terrified him but what was worse was the fact that he knew he could do nothing about it.

As the aircraft gained height, the air grew noticeably colder. Jacob began to shiver. He felt his face. His cheeks were icy to the touch. When he breathed out a mist formed briefly in front of his face. At the same time he found it was becoming harder to breathe. He hunched himself up, clutching his knees to his chin, hoping this might conserve his body warmth. It did not. He felt his toes growing numb despite the two layers of socks. His fingers also started to tingle with pins and needles and his eyes stung. For a short while he found it difficult to concentrate on anything. His mind started to wander, and there was a voice at the back of his head bizarrely telling him it was only an hour to go to milking.

Finally the Lysander settled once more into an even flight path, slowly descending. Gradually Jacob felt his body warming slightly, his breathing coming easier. Rubbing his bruises, he watched the land beneath move infinitesimally up towards the aircraft.

There were farms and villages below but they were farther apart than in England and there was much more woodland. In places it stretched for miles. Flying up to a river, the Lysander banked to the right and began to follow its valley, the water a streak of tarnished silver in the darkness of the night.

Taking Jacob by surprise, the Lysander suddenly banked sharply again, its wing dipping to the land below which seemed to consist of fields surrounded by patch-works of forest. In a large clearing were three lights in the shape of an inverted L. At the bottom of the long arm was a red light: the other two were white. One of them winked briefly. The aircraft overflew the site once, rose, turned at a tight angle and descended steeply, the engine almost idling, its noise replaced now by the rush of wind.

Jacob held on to the netting. The front wheels of the Lysander touched the ground, stones rattling up against the fuselage. Very quickly the aircraft slowed, the tail dropping. It swung round through 180 degrees. The engine was cut. Only the swishing of the freewheeling propeller broke the silence.

Now, Jacob thought, was the tricky part.

Running footsteps approached the Lysander. Jacob could hear muffled voices speaking urgently in both English and French.

'*Bonsoir*, Wing Commander. *Comment allez-vous?*' The voice spoke in an undertone.

'*Je suis bien.*' It was the pilot's voice. 'We must be quick.'

'*Oui.* Five minutes, *m'sieur.* You 'ave something for us?'

Five minutes, Jacob thought. He would have to move soon.

'Indeed, André, I have. On the seat. London has also sent some other supplies. Stens and PE.'

'*Très bien, n'est-ce pas?*'

'*Non! C'est magnifique!*' another voice declared emphatically and with evident glee.

The aircraft rocked on its wheels as someone climbed the ladder and opened the rear canopy. Jacob pressed himself against the rear bulkhead. He had wondered if he should hide in the space behind it but thought it would take him too long to get out. Better, he decided, to chance it in the compartment.

Someone leaned over the rim of the canopy, grabbed the briefcase and black leather bag and jumped down. The moon had set and he was little more than a black ghost in the darkness. More footsteps approached the aircraft.

'Wing Commander Pickering?' It was a male voice, quiet, reserved, English.

'Yes,' the pilot confirmed. 'You must be Gladiator. I'm glad you made it safely.'

'Unlike some.' There was a pause. 'Unfortunately there's no news of our radio operator, Valerian.'

Jacob felt the hairs on the nape of his neck prickle. This man knew his mother.

It was time to move. Grasping hold of his satchel, Jacob risked a peek over the rim of the canopy. The pilot and the Englishman were speaking on the opposite side of the fuselage from the ladder. Another man, holding a rifle across his chest, stood sentry by the engine facing the distant trees. Two others were examining the contents of the briefcase, removing documents from it and folding them into their pockets. A fourth was walking across the field of stubble and short grass in which the Lysander had landed, leading a pony and cart.

As quickly and as quietly as he could, Jacob swung his legs over the side of the aircraft, felt for the ladder with his foot, found it and descended to the ground. By now the man and the cart were much nearer. To his dismay Jacob could see nowhere to hide. For a hundred metres in every direction there was nothing but short stubble.

'Pierre!' the approaching man said. '*Viens ici . . .*'

The man with the rifle turned. Jacob instinctively lowered himself to the earth like a rabbit caught out in the open: if he had long ears, he thought, he would flatten them.

Step by step they drew nearer still. Any second, Jacob was sure he would be seen. He eased himself along the ground away from the foot of the ladder, towards the rear of the aircraft, lying down under the short tail planes.

'*Vite! Vite!*' the newcomer exclaimed.

The four Frenchmen set about unloading the Lysander, piling its cargo into the cart. As soon as the compartment was empty, a small suitcase was dropped into it and the Englishman climbed aboard. The pilot returned to the cockpit. The pony and cart set off heading for the woods.

'*Au revoir*, Wing Commander!' André announced, raising his hand in a farewell wave. '*Bon voyage – et merci beaucoup.*'

There was a brief whine, the propeller turned jerkily then the engine caught. Noxious black smoke erupted from the exhaust pipes, taking Jacob by surprise and engulfing him. A fierce wind blew over him and the tail wheel began to move, turning towards his head. He quickly rolled over. The Lysander accelerated away from him and took off, as invisible as a bat against the night sky.

By now the Frenchmen were almost at the edge of

the trees, following the cart. Jacob stood up, hurriedly brushed a scattering of stubble stalks from his clothing and set off after them, his satchel in his hand. When he came to the verge of the wood, the men were nowhere in sight but he discovered a narrow trail overgrown by grass leading through the trees, dense foliage on either side. The grass was flattened in two lines by the cart wheels.

It was darker beneath the trees than it had been in the stubble field and, despite Jacob's eyes being accustomed to the night, he still found it hard to avoid tripping over ruts or tree roots. Twice he wandered off the path into bushes and had to backtrack, his hands scratched by briars.

He must have gone about half a kilometre when he arrived in a clearing. In the centre was a low, derelict cottage. The roof had fallen in and creepers wound themselves around the exposed beams. The track passed close to the building before turning at an angle to avoid a forest pool.

At the sight of the water, Jacob realized he was thirsty. The last drink he had had was the glass of milk in his bedroom and that seemed a lifetime ago. Determined to preserve the water in the hip flask, he put down his satchel, knelt at the edge of the pool and, cupping his hands, bent to drink.

Something cold and hard suddenly jabbed into the back of his neck, almost pitching him forwards into the water. A tidal wave of terror surged through him. It was like having ice crystals form on his bones.

'*Qu'est-que vous?*' a voice muttered.

Jacob, pushing his hands into the sodden peaty earth,

tried to get up, twisting his head to see who was behind him. The muzzle of a gun slid round his neck to press into his cheek, turning his face. He could smell the gun oil and feel it smear his skin.

'*Ne bougez pas!*'

He did not understand what was being said to him but, he considered, at least the voice was speaking French, not German. Despite this, staring at the black water, the thought occurred to him that he might at any moment be forced under it, to drown.

'I am – *je suis* – English,' he said.

There was a stunned silence.

'*Anglais!*' someone exclaimed.

The gun muzzle was withdrawn. Jacob heard the safely catch metallically click on. Several other men came over to him, their boots squelching in the waterlogged earth.

'Inglish?' another voice asked, incredulously.

La Tour was a square three-storey tower, once part of a small chateau most of which had long since fallen into disrepair and existed only as ruins. In front of it were the remains of a cobbled courtyard surrounded by fallen stone walls. About half a kilometre from a village, it was built of grey stone with a slate roof, on the side of a hill overlooking a wide, slow-moving river traversed near the village by an ancient bridge. The door was heavy and studded with iron bolts, the windows narrow. The main room, on the ground floor, contained a huge fireplace, some upright chairs and an oak table so old it was black. In the fireplace was a cast-iron range. A wooden trapdoor in the flagstone floor led down to a mildewed cellar lined with empty wine bottle racks. Over the main room, approached by woodworm-riddled stairs, were two other chambers one above the other, the lower containing a double bed with an iron frame and a rickety chest of drawers, the upper bare of any furniture save a wooden chair.

Next to the tower was a cottage, the only inhabitable part left of the chateau.

By the time Jacob woke in the morning, the sun was well up and shining across the foot of the bed. On the chest of drawers someone had placed a basin, a ewer of hot water and a towel. Leaning against it was his satchel. He washed his face and hands then, as he was still wearing everything he had flown in, he undressed and put on clean clothes. Running his fingers through his hair, he looked out of the window. In the far distance were woods. Closer to the tower was a vineyard, an apple orchard, a field of what looked like wheat and a rank pasture of long grass.

Opening the door, he went down the stairs to discover a fire had been lit in the range. An elderly woman in a shawl was heating a pan of water on the ring.

'Good morning,' she said, not turning round.

'Good morning,' Jacob replied.

The woman dipped a ladle into the pan, removed two eggs and set them in two silver eggcups.

'I am Madame Aubry,' the woman introduced herself in perfect English. 'What is your name?'

'Jacob Adams.'

'Well, Jacob, you sit here and eat your breakfast and then we shall talk.'

She placed the eggs on the table and, handing Jacob a teaspoon, sat down opposite him. Thanking her, he cracked open the eggs. The yolk was runny but the white firm. They did not taste like those at home and he assumed it was because French chickens ate different weeds from English ones. When he had finished, Madame Aubry removed the eggcups and, giving Jacob a mug of warm milk, leaned forward to rest her arms on the table.

'Now, you must know some things, Jacob Adams,' she announced sternly, staring him in the eye. 'You have been a foolish — a *very* foolish — boy. By stowing yourself away on the aircraft you have put not only yourself but many other people in great danger. Just your being here is a risk. If the Germans come here and find you, I will be arrested. Maybe shot. The men who brought you here also have their lives in jeopardy by your presence.'

Jacob sipped the milk. It was creamy and thick.

'Do you not know France is occupied by the Nazis?' Madame Aubry continued. 'The war for you in England is across the sea, but for us in France it is here, in our gardens, in our houses, in the streets of our villages and towns. People are killed here. This is no place and no time for childish pranks.'

Madame Aubry's lecture made Jacob feel guilty yet, at the same time, he was stung by her words.

'Hiding in the Lysander was no prank,' Jacob retorted, defending himself, 'and I do know France is occupied and the war is not so far away for us in England. The cities are bombed almost every night. We see the bombers going overhead.'

It occurred to him then that he might not be able to trust Madame Aubry. He knew nothing of her. She might be one of those Quislings his grandfather had mentioned. On the other hand, he reasoned, the men who had met the Lysander had brought him here so they must trust her.

'My father is fighting in India,' Jacob went on 'and my mother is here in France.' He paused then, casting aside his uncertainty, added, 'My mother's real name is Barbara but here in France they call her Valerian.'

Madame Aubry stared at Jacob. As if in slow motion, she put her hand to her mouth, exclaiming quietly, '*Mon Dieu!*'

'Do you know my mother?' Jacob asked.

For a moment, Madame Aubry said nothing then, quite emphatically, she said, 'Yes. I know your mother.'

With that she rose swiftly to her feet and, leaving the tower, closed the door behind her. Jacob finished the milk but his hand was shaking. If she was not to be trusted, he was now doomed.

In a few minutes she returned with a handful of clothes and a wicker sewing basket which she put on the table.

'Jacob,' she announced with some urgency, 'your life – and ours – depends upon obedience. Like a soldier, you will obey orders. You understand?'

'Yes,' Jacob said, wondering what was coming next.

'Good,' Madame Aubry replied. She briefly smiled at him, putting him at his ease. 'Now, take all your clothes off. Everything. And put these on.' She indicated the pile on the table. 'They belong to my nephew. He is about your size. Your clothing looks too English. Now you must look like a French boy.' She turned her back on him.

Jacob got undressed. As he took off his clothes, Madame Aubry turned each garment inside out and deftly cut out all the labels with a pair of nail scissors. She dropped them in the range to burn.

'Why are you doing that?' Jacob asked as he tugged on a pair of brown moleskin trousers.

'If the Germans find these . . .' she said, then she shrugged. 'Without labels, what can they know?'

'I've some other clothes,' Jacob admitted.

'I'll see to them,' Madame Aubry replied.

When Jacob was dressed again, Madame Aubry stepped back and studied him. She nodded approvingly.

'Now, Jacob,' she asked. 'Do you speak French?'

'Not really,' Jacob admitted. 'I've just started to learn it in school.' He began to recite the verb *être*. '*Je suis, tu es, il est, elle est, nous sommes . . .*'

Madame Aubry interrupted him, raising her hand.

'Come!' she said, lifting the trapdoor in the floor and going down the steps into the cellar, Jacob following her. 'Watch.'

From the top of the wine racks, she picked up a thin steel rod the size of a knitting needle and inserted it into a tiny hole between two stones. There was a muffled click. She extracted the rod and a section of the wall swung open.

'This was a passage under the ground, from the days of the Revolution,' she explained. 'It went to the chateau but now it has collapsed some way along. This matters not. Listen to me. If someone comes when you are in the tower alone, you must hide here.' She picked up a torch from a niche in the wall of the passage and switched it on. Jacob could see some boxes stacked against the walls. 'Do not worry about air in the tunnel. There are holes. Remember to take the rod in with you, then no one may follow you even if he knows of this tunnel. To open from within,' she pointed to a lever on the inside of the door, 'push this up. But,' she wagged her finger to emphasize her point, 'do not come out until you hear three knocks then two knocks on the wall.' She demonstrated the signal with her knuckles. 'You understand?'

It was Jacob's turn to nod.

'You can go out of the tower but do not leave the courtyard. If someone sees you and comes while you are outside, go into the orchard, to the farthest trees. There the grass is long. Lie down and wait. Do not go into the tower and hide. And,' she added, 'if you need to use the lavatory, go into my cottage.'

'Why can't I hide in the tunnel?' Jacob enquired.

'If they see you come in and follow you and do not find you, they will know there is a hiding place and they will search.'

'What are in the boxes?'

Madame Aubry looked hard at Jacob and said, 'You ask too many questions. If you were a French boy, rather than just looked like one, I might be worried.'

This puzzled Jacob and he asked, 'Why?'

'Not all French people are as they seem. Some are collaborators who help the Nazis.' She swung the door shut and the mechanism clicked in place. When it was closed, the door was indiscernible from the surrounding wall. 'The boxes contain guns and ammunition,' she said bluntly.

'Are they for the Resistance?' Jacob asked.

Madame Aubry stared at him. For a moment she was speechless. Then she said, 'How do you know of this?'

'Grampy – my grandfather – told me. They cut telephone lines and gather intelligence. Are you . . .?' he ventured.

'Yes,' Madame Aubry replied, returning the rod to the top of the bottle racks. 'I am one of them.'

She turned and went up the steps into the main room. She folded Jacob's shirt, vest and pullovers and gathered them into a pile.

'Did the guns come in the Lysander?'

'Not last night,' Madame Aubry answered. 'A month ago.'

Jacob thought for a moment then asked, 'Did my mother come in a Lysander?'

Madame Aubry took Jacob's hand and stroked it. 'Just like you. The very same aircraft.'

'Do you know where she is?'

Madame Aubry did not immediately reply. She let go of Jacob's hand and picked up her sewing basket.

'I have to go,' she announced. 'You will stay here. Let the stove go out. If you want water, go to the well outside. And be on your guard. I will return in two hours.'

With that, she left the tower. Jacob went up to the top storey and looked out. Halfway down the hill, he could see Madame Aubry hurriedly making her way along a path towards the village.

Shortly before midday, the latch on the door lifted. Jacob, who had left the tower only once since Madame Aubry's departure, to go to her cottage, was back on the top floor, keeping himself occupied by maintaining a lookout. Yet, despite the fact that windows faced in all directions and he had constantly moved from one to another, he had seen no one approach. Descending to the cellar was out of the question. To get there, he would have to have passed through the main, ground floor room. Whoever had entered the building was sure to be in there.

Jacob waited with bated breath. Perhaps, he reasoned, whoever it was would believe the place empty and leave. The thought had no sooner come to him, however, than he heard footsteps on the stairs. His knees felt weak. He tried to get a grip on himself but could not. Every nerve in his body was as tight as a tambourine skin.

The steps halted on the floor below. Jacob imagined a German soldier standing there, his square helmet on his head, his rifle at the ready, the bayonet fixed and catching the sunlight from the window. He was studying the room, his head tilted as he listened for some tell-tale sound. Then his hand reached out and picked up the pullover Jacob had left on the chair. He held it close to his face, sniffing at it as an animal would, running his finger along the neck in search of the label . . .

This terrifying daydream was interrupted by someone tapping on the table: *knock-knock-knock*, pause, *knock-knock*. Tentatively, Jacob went to the head of the staircase and looked down. Standing in the middle of the room below was a man wearing a shabby jacket and a black beret.

'Ah!' he remarked, as if surprised to see Jacob. 'There you are. Come on down. It's quite safe.'

When Jacob reached the ground floor, he found the man seated at the table on which stood a bottle of wine and two glasses.

'Hello, Jacob,' he said. 'Do take a seat.' He indicated a chair and reached for the bottle which had already been uncorked. 'If you're to be a real French boy, we'd best treat you like one.' He poured out two glasses of wine, pushing one across to Jacob. 'French lads drink wine.'

'My grandfather lets me have a glass of cider at lunch-time,' Jacob stated. 'He says it will put hairs on my chest.'

'This is a Beaujolais,' the man replied, 'and it will not contribute to your hirsute characteristics.' He held his glass up. '*Vive la France!*'

'*Vive la France!*' Jacob repeated, although he did not know exactly what it meant, and he sipped the wine. It had a grainy taste which he did not find pleasant.

'What I'm going to tell you,' the man continued, 'can go no further than this room and you would not be privy to it, I can assure you, were it not you know so much already. Madame Aubry has told me who you are and I can guess why you are here, although how you found out about the current situation is presently beyond me.' He took another sip of wine. 'What you've done is down-right foolhardy – she's told you as much – but I can see your motive and I have to admit that, just as there is a very thin line between genius and madness, so is there between foolishness and courage. You have shown great courage and I admire you for it, but that doesn't mean it wasn't also a remarkably stupid thing to do.'

49

As he spoke, Jacob noticed the man's jacket had fallen open. Under his armpit, he could see the polished wooden butt of a revolver nestling in a leather shoulder holster.

'You will be wondering who I am and what I am,' the man went on. 'I cannot tell you my real name, only that by which I am known here.'

'Your code name,' Jacob interrupted.

'So, you know about code names too,' the man replied pensively.

'My mother is Valerian.'

'Indeed she is, but keep that to yourself. The less you seem to know, the better it will be for you. As for myself, I am code-named Mercator. That is all you need to know and all I am prepared to tell you. As for what I am, I am sure you have a shrewd idea.'

As Mercator took another sip of wine, Jacob studied him. He looked almost down and out. His beret was stained, his shirt was grimy and had no collar, his jacket was frayed at the cuffs, his trousers were baggy at the knees and his shoes had not been polished in ages. His chin bore a shadow of stubble and his fingernails were dirty. Whatever he looked like, it was neither a soldier nor a fighter: indeed, Jacob considered, he was more like an elderly professional man – a doctor or a solicitor – who had taken to the bottle and gone to seed or been interrupted in his gardening clothes.

'Are you English?'

Mercator smiled and said, 'As English as the Union Jack and the Grand Old Duke of York.'

'You don't look English,' Jacob ventured, 'or very . . .'

'Sartorially elegant,' Mercator butted in. 'But I blend

in. That,' he added pointedly, 'is why I'm still alive.' He picked up the bottle, replaced the cork and slid it into his jacket pocket. 'I see you're not partial to Beaujolais. Next time we'll try Vouvray.'

From outside came a low cough, like someone clearing their throat.

In an instant Jacob's nerves were on edge.

'It's all right,' Mercator said, recognizing Jacob's alarm, 'and it's good you are alert. That is Guillaume. He's the one who brought you here in the night. Now,' he went on, 'you will stay here until another Lysander flight is scheduled. You will return on that. Don't worry about getting into trouble when you get back. While your behaviour has hardly been – how shall I put it? – circumspect, people will understand in the circumstances. It's more important you don't get into trouble here.'

'When will the Lysander come?'

'When we need it,' Mercator replied, 'or London wishes to send it.'

'Must I stay here all the time?' Jacob asked.

'Yes,' Mercator replied categorically. 'This is a dangerous place. *Everywhere*,' he emphasized, 'has danger inherent in it. It may all seem like an adventure to you, but to us . . . Any hour of any day may be our last. We are running a perilous game here of cat and mouse and,' he added, almost as an afterthought, 'sabotage.'

The door opened a few centimetres and a voice from outside murmured, '*Il est temps de partir, m'sieur.*'

Mercator pushed back his frayed jacket cuff and glanced at his watch. 'I have something to which I must attend,' he said. 'Madame Aubry will look after you. Do everything she says. To the letter. Got it?'

'Got it,' Jacob confirmed.

Yet there was still another question Jacob had to ask. It burned in him like a dull, persistent pain deep down inside him, churning away at his soul. He looked Mercator straight in the eye.

'Is my mother still alive?'

'Yes,' Mercator replied, without hesitation.

'Where is she?'

Mercator considered for a moment then said, 'She was arrested last week. By the Gestapo. That's the German secret police. At present she is being held in the Gestapo headquarters in a town ten kilometres away.'

4

As soon as Mercator had departed, Jacob left the tower and walked into the orchard. Most of the trees were heavy with unripe fruit. In the grass, crickets chirruped. Lizards were sunning themselves on a pile of stones dumped under an ancient pear tree. As he approached they scattered for cover, their green bodies flicking out of sight.

Choosing a patch of grass well away from the tower, Jacob sat down and opened the AA roadmap book he had brought with him. Turning to the back, he ran his finger down the index. He knew what he was looking for: when he had entered Madame Aubry's cottage to use the lavatory, he had seen a telephone. Behind a small glass circle in the centre of the dial was the number – and the name of the telephone exchange. All he had to do was discover the place on the map and he would know where he was but, when his finger found the name – Belmont – his heart sank. There were nineteen of them.

One by one, Jacob looked them up, his spirits rising with each discovery. When he had located them all, he found only two were close to rivers, but one of these was in south-eastern France, at least 550 miles in a straight line from the English coast. Knowing the Lysander's top speed to be only just over 200 miles an hour, and that the flight had lasted only an hour and a half, he considered it stood to reason that he must be in the other Belmont. Using a long blade of grass as a ruler, he measured the distance against the scale at the foot of the page. As near as made no difference, it was 300 miles.

Elated, Jacob studied the map. Sure enough, there was a large town, just as Mercator had said there was. According to the scale, it was ten kilometres – or six miles – down the river. That, he was certain, was where his mother was being held.

Returning to the tower, Jacob checked that Madame Aubry had not returned. He went into her cottage and, finding a piece of onionskin paper and a pencil in a writing desk, quickly traced the area of map between Belmont and the town. Hiding the book under the mattress of his bed, he left the tower and struck off through the vineyard, where the vines were hung with heavy bunches of reddening grapes. At the far side was a well-worn path heading down the hill towards the river. Checking no one was in sight, Jacob set off along it.

The sun was warm, the ground dry and dusty, the air almost golden. Butterflies hovered above small ox-eye daisies on the edge of a wheat field. At one point, as the path dipped sharply towards the river, Jacob saw an adder on a smooth stone, but it quickly slithered away at his approach.

The path ended at a roadway running along the bank of the river. Jacob waited for a few minutes, listening for any vehicles and keeping a lookout. Finally he stepped out into the road and headed off in the direction of the town.

For two hours he walked at a brisk pace. Only twice did he see a vehicle. The first was a rattling Citroën lorry loaded with empty apple boxes, the second a nondescript black saloon driven by an elderly woman in a straw hat. On neither occasion did Jacob either hide or wave. To have done so would have attracted attention. Although the road went by several houses and farms, Jacob saw nobody else except a man in the yard of one of the farms, repairing a horse-drawn threshing machine. He did not look up from his work.

Eventually Jacob reached his destination. The town was not as large as he had expected, little more than a small market town of perhaps a hundred houses gathered around a tree-lined central square in which there stood the town hall, a butcher's shop with not a single piece of meat, a baker's with only three loaves of bread, and several other shops all of which were shut. Across the square from the town hall was a café, its scrubbed wooden tables arranged outside on the cobbles, in the shade of the trees. Beyond it, down a short street, was a bridge over the river.

Jacob stood at a corner, close into the wall and surveyed the scene. As he did so, the clock on the town hall chimed three. The square was deserted, almost every window shuttered against the hot afternoon sun. A sleeping cat lay curled on the bonnet of a Peugeot van, the only vehicle in sight. Sparrows chirped in the trees. After a few minutes, a waiter came out of the café, a white apron tied round his waist. He cursorily wiped one of the tables, looking round as he did so as if willing a customer to appear. As if to grant his wish, an elderly man shambling along with the aid of a stick materialized from a side street. However, instead of heading for the café, he went into the *pissoir*. Jacob could see his shoes through the gap under the wall as he urinated. After a minute he stepped out, doing up his fly buttons, and went back the way he had come.

As resolutely as he could, Jacob set off across the square. He knew he looked like a French boy but that did not prevent him feeling as if every shuttered window hid eyes that were watching his progress.

Halfway across, he paused to look down towards the river. At the beginning of the bridge was a barrier painted in red and white stripes. Next to it was a wall of sandbags on the top of which was positioned a heavy machine-gun, the barrel resting upon a bipod and pointing directly into the square. Beside it stood four German soldiers. Their grey uniforms were almost the same colour as the bridge, the silver insignia on their collars and eagles over their right breast pockets glinting in the sun. One held a rifle while the other three smoked cigarettes and chatted.

Jacob felt a frisson of fear rip up his spine. Not a hundred metres away was the enemy. He wanted to take to his heels, sprint for cover. Yet to do so, he knew, would be to risk inviting a fusillade of shots. Taking hold of himself, he continued at a measured pace across the square and into a side street which, according to a white and blue plaque, was called Rue Puget.

Once out of the Germans' sight, Jacob felt weak. He leaned against a wall and tried to compose himself. His heart was thumping hard and his forehead was bathed in sweat. The palms of his hands felt clammy.

Suddenly, from a doorway, appeared the shambling old man holding a glass of water in a trembling hand.

'*Il fait chaud*,' he remarked in a wavering, croaky voice, looking up at the sky and shielding his eyes with his other hand. '*Voici un boisson.*' He smiled and offered the glass to Jacob. '*C'est de l'eau, très froide.*'

Jacob accepted the glass and drained it in one. The water was so cold it made his head swim.

The old man looked down the street in the direction of the square. He glowered and muttered, '*Les Boche!*' He spat vehemently on to the pavement. '*Ils sont des animaux!*'

Giving him the glass back, Jacob said, '*Merci beaucoup, monsieur*', one of the few phrases he knew in French.

The old man gave him a long, quizzical look. It was then Jacob realized his accent must have been far from that of a French schoolboy. For a moment he was very afraid: what if the old man was a collaborator? However, instead of grabbing Jacob by the arm and dragging him off to the Nazis, the old man grinned expansively and, reaching into his pocket, produced a handful of coins. Putting the glass on a window sill, he opened Jacob's hand, dropped the coins into it and closed his fingers around them. Then he winked, picked up the glass, entered his house and closed the door.

As he walked on, Jacob cursed himself. It was a stupid mistake. He might just as well as have said, 'Thank you very much, sir'. From now on he resolved not to speak, even if addressed. He would play the idiot. It was, he thought, better to keep his mouth shut and be thought a fool, than open his mouth and prove it.

The side street gave on to a wider thoroughfare of imposing residential terraced houses. Another white and blue sign on a wall gave its name – Boulevard Descartes.

Like most of the town, the buildings dated back at least a century, some with grand flights of steps up from the street, several with little crescent-shaped lay-bys for carriages. A number had iron railings and ornate gas lamps. Yet it was not the architecture that captured Jacob's attention. It was a building halfway down the street. Five storeys high, with a leaded roof set in with a row of dormer windows, its façade was draped with a red and black Nazi flag emblazoned with the swastika. At the foot of the steps stood two German sentries. Both were armed with sub-machine guns. To one side, a black Mercedes-Benz staff car was parked, a uniformed driver avidly polishing the paintwork. For fifty metres on either side, the trees that lined the boulevard had been felled to stumps to give the sentries and, Jacob considered, men at the windows, a clear line of fire if the building were to be attacked.

This building, Jacob reasoned, had to be the German forces' local headquarters. It therefore followed that was where his mother was being imprisoned.

Edging into the shadow of a flight of steps leading up to a rather imposing if rundown mansion, Jacob peered through a stone balustrade at the Gestapo headquarters. There was only one entrance at the front but, he noticed, a narrow alley seemed to run down one side, separating the building from its neighbour. He knew he had to find out what was in it.

Taking a deep breath, as if he was about to plunge into deep water, Jacob moved out from behind the balustrade and started down the boulevard. He walked with a measured pace, not too fast, not too slow. Every step brought him nearer and nearer to the sentries. Thirty metres from the entrance, one of the sentries turned and watched him, his face shaded by the square edge of his grey helmet. Jacob caught sight of his finger as it moved from the trigger guard to the trigger of his sub-machine gun.

Jacob carried on, fighting the fear mounting in him. At last he reached the alleyway and glanced down it. It led from the boulevard to another street. He turned and walked towards it. The sentry did not take his eyes off him. Just as he was about to enter the alley, a guttural voice shouted at him.

'*Halt!*'

The command was followed by the sound of army boots on cobbles. Jacob froze. The soldier came right up to him. '*Wo willst du denn hin?*'

Slowly, Jacob turned to face him. Deciding idiocy to be the better part of valour, he put on what he hoped was a simpleton's gawp.

'*Hau ab!*' the soldier said curtly, signalling Jacob away from the entrance to the alley with the barrel of the sub-machine gun.

Jacob watched, almost entranced, as the sunlight glanced off the gunmetal. This, he thought distantly, was what it must be like to be a rabbit held in the gaze of a stoat. Making a little bow of obedience, he complied and set off to retrace his steps down the boulevard.

'*Was ist es, Hans?*' he heard the second sentry enquire.

'*Französisches Blag!*' came the contemptuous reply.

Although he no idea what it meant, Jacob could guess it was not complimentary.

Once of out sight of the building, his face broke into a wide, self-congratulatory grin. He had only had a moment to take in the alley but, in those few seconds, he had seen what he wanted. Set into the cobbles a quarter of the way along was a circular iron cover. It was a coal hole and beneath it, Jacob knew, there would be a coal cellar.

When Jacob reached the square, little had changed in it. The cat was still asleep on the van bonnet. The birds still sang in the trees. However, at one of the tables outside the café sat three German officers. Like the soldiers guarding the bridge, their uniforms were grey and well tailored, their black riding boots and leather pistol holsters highly polished. On their tunic collars were black squares containing what looked from a distance to be a maple leaf in silver braid. One wore a black and silver Iron Cross at his throat. They had placed their peaked caps on the table before them and were talking.

Despite himself, Jacob walked towards the café. This trio of smartly dressed men held a strange and deadly fascination for him. The nearer he drew to them, the more they looked no different from any other army officer. Even his father. They had an officer's bearing about them, an indefinable charisma, a presence of power. Yet it was bizarre to think that, were they to know who he was, they would kill him with no more thought than they would swat a wasp at a picnic.

The waiter came out of the café carrying a tray upon

which were three glasses of water and three of Pernod. As he placed these upon the table, he gave Jacob a brief fleeting glance then looked up at the clock on the town hall.

Closer still, Jacob could see the detail on their caps. Each was grey, decorated with silver cords, an eagle in silver braid sewn above a silver skull-and-crossbones. The sight of this grotesque symbol of death brought Jacob to his senses. These were not officers like his father but men for whom all human life was cheap.

'Marcel!'

The waiter, having served the Germans, came walking briskly across the square towards Jacob.

'*Ça va, Marcel?*' he said jovially to Jacob, smiling broadly. '*Pourquoi tu n'es pas à l'école, cet après-midi?*'

Much to Jacob's consternation, the waiter took him by the hand and began to lead him towards the café. He could hardly resist, the waiter's grip was so firm.

'*Une glace, Jacob? Un jus d'orange, peut-être?*'

Bustling him right past the German officers, who paid not the slightest attention to either of them, the waiter led Jacob into the café and round to the rear of the bar. An older man, whom Jacob assumed was the café proprietor, was standing there gazing out of the window, absent-mindedly drying a wine glass with a cloth.

'*Pierre, il est quatre heures moins cinq,*' the older man murmured, putting the glass and cloth on the bar.

'*Oui . . .*'

Together the two men crouched down behind the bar counter. The waiter put his hand on Jacob's shoulder, pulling him down with them.

'I,' he said in broken English, 'Pierre. You forget, yes? I was at Lysander. You down, boy, down.'

Outside, Jacob could hear the German officers laughing.

Suddenly there was a squealing of tyres and the noise of a car engine in the square. It was immediately followed by the sharp rattle of automatic weapons. They sounded no louder than fireworks going off. The window of the café shattered, the glass crashing to the floor. At the end of the bar, on a shelf, an earthenware bottle of liqueur exploded, peppering Jacob with shards of pottery and showering him with a sticky green liquid that smelt strongly of mint.

Over this cacophony came the racing of the car engine as it careered out of the square and round the corner towards the bridge. There was another more distant burst of gunfire, then what seemed to be complete and utter silence.

The two Frenchmen stood up and solemnly shook hands. There was a look of resolute satisfaction on their faces. Jacob peered over the bar and out through where the window had been. Several of the tables and chairs outside were in splinters. Others were strewn about on their sides. One table was riddled with holes. A thin blue mist eddied in the air, rising and drifting away in the branches of the trees. Leaves drifted down, cut loose by ricochets.

One of the German officers lay on his back, his body twitching spasmodically. His outstretched hand opened and closed as if trying to grasp the life that was ebbing away from him. Beyond him, one of the other two was hunched up in an expanding puddle of blood that was beginning to flow between the cobbles towards a drain. The third was sprawled across a table, his skull split open. Jacob could see where a spongy tissue had leaked out of the wound.

He knew what he was looking at, yet it was several seconds before Jacob was struck by the enormity of the scene. This was not a gangster film, not even a Pathé newsreel of the war showing before the main feature in the half-light of the Majestic cinema. This was reality. He had just seen three men killed in cold blood. Forty-five seconds ago, they had been drinking Pernod and laughing. Now they were twitching and bleeding to death on the cobbles, or lay with their brains smeared across a scrubbed wooden table.

'You go!' Pierre muttered urgently, interrupting his thoughts.

He guided Jacob through a store room behind the bar and out into an alley behind, wiping the drink off him with his apron as they went.

'*Merci* . . .' Jacob said. He wanted to say more but found he could not. It was not that he did not know any more French words – which, in fact, he didn't – but that, even in English, nothing appropriate would come to mind.

'*C'est bien,*' Pierre replied then, pointing to the far end of the alley, added, 'This way go. No stop.'

Keeping to side streets, Jacob was soon at the edge of the town. Behind him, he could hear shouting, punctuated by sporadic gunfire. Checking the road was clear, he set off at a jog. On several occasions vehicles came speeding along the road but he managed to step into the bushes or a ditch before they reached him. It was getting

63

on for six o'clock when he reached the pathway and set off up the hill towards La Tour.

When Jacob arrived at the tower it seemed deserted. The courtyard was still, the shadows lengthening as evening drew on. Swallows dipped to a nest of mud and straw glued to the wall beneath the eaves of the tower roof. Jacob opened the door of the tower and entered quietly, closing the door behind him. The range had been lit and a kettle was simmering on the hob. Upon the table a place had been set for one, a plate of cold meat and several tomatoes between a knife and fork, a tumbler of water and some bread. Realizing now that he was hungry, Jacob was wondering if he should sit down and eat as the door opened and Mercator came in, a Sten machine-carbine held in the crook of his arm. Behind him came Madame Aubry.

'Where the bloody hell do you think you've been?' Mercator snapped.

'I went to the town,' Jacob admitted.

'That much we know,' Mercator replied tersely. 'We've had a telephone call from Pierre. If it hadn't been for him, you'd now be lying in the town square next to three SS officers.' He put the Sten down on the table. 'You've no idea how close you came to jeopardizing an operation that's been in the planning for weeks.'

'I'm sorry,' Jacob apologized. 'I only wanted to see where my mother was.'

'"You only wanted,"' Mercator repeated. 'This war

isn't about you. You can't let matters get personal in a war.'

'I can,' Jacob responded. 'It's my mother they've got.'

Mercator looked at Madame Aubry for a moment then said, 'Jacob, sit down and have your supper.'

While Jacob ate, Mercator and Madame Aubry went outside. He could hear them talking in low tones. Just as Jacob finished they came back in. Mercator sat across the table from him, with Madame Aubry by his side. She took away the empty plate and glass and put a bottle of wine in their place with three glasses. Mercator, however, only filled two of them, passing one to Madame Aubry and keeping the second for himself.

'Do you know how long it takes to lull three senior German officers into a false sense of security?' Mercator asked. 'Six months,' he added, not waiting for an answer. 'Six months of serving them glasses of Pernod and cups of coffee, smiling at them, waiving the bill and feeding them croissants and pieces of true but valueless information.'

'You must understand, Jacob,' Madame Aubry said, 'in the war we are fighting, there are not Spitfires and bombers, big targets or armies facing each other across a battlefield. For us, our battlefield is every street corner, every café, every road. Our best weapon is not this –' she laid her hand briefly on the Sten '– but surprise. Even here, in La Tour, you are not safe.'

'What Madame Aubry is saying,' Mercator interjected, 'is that what might look like a calm countryside in summer is actually a place where, at any second, the war may strike. You just don't seem able to comprehend the predicament we – and you – are in.'

Mercator sipped at his wine. Jacob wondered if he was

going to be offered a glass. Madame Aubry got up and put more wood in the stove.

'I'm sorry,' Jacob admitted a second time. 'I do understand but . . .' His voice tailed off. There seemed nothing else he could say.

'We'll talk no more about it,' Mercator said, leaning forward. 'I have news of your mother.'

'Is she in that building on Boulevard Descartes?' Jacob asked.

'Yes. She is being held in a room on the top floor. But,' he went on, 'we know from an informant that they are going to move her over the next few days. We don't know exactly when yet.'

'Move her?'

'They will take her to Germany,' Madame Aubry said.

Jacob felt a cold numbness spreading through him. 'Is she all right?' he asked.

'They've been interrogating her for over a week,' Mercator answered ominously. 'That can mean any-thing.'

Madame Aubry sat down again and put her arm round Jacob. 'Try not to worry,' she said softly, 'but be prepared. And be brave. This is how it is.'

Jacob's eyes started to sting. He could feel the tears beginning to well up. Madame Aubry produced a cotton handkerchief and dabbed his cheek.

'If you to want to cry, *mon cheri*, you just do it,' she whispered.

Yet Jacob did not. He fought back the tears. It was no use crying. Crying would not rescue his mother. Resolve would.

Mercator said, 'I admire your pluck, Jacob. There's

not many boys would risk what you have. But you can't carry on going off at half-cock. A loose cannon. We – and that now includes you – will only achieve our goal if we act together. With discipline.' His voice became businesslike. 'You're here for a few more days yet and you've shown to Madame and me that you've got guts. Got what it takes. And you've successfully passed yourself off as a French lad right under the noses of the enemy.' He paused. 'What do you think, Madame?'

'I think yes,' Madame Aubry replied.

'Very well,' Mercator continued and he leaned back in his chair, calling, 'Emile . . .'

There was a scuffling on the floor above and a young man appeared, helped down the stairs by a Frenchman with another Sten slung over his shoulder. The young man was dressed in a leather flying jacket, the left leg of his trousers ripped and ragged. His face was pale, there was a gash across his forehead above his right eye, which had been bleeding, and he limped badly.

'This is Flight Lieutenant Bax,' Mercator announced. 'His Halifax was shot down two nights ago and now he's going down the line.'

Emile helped the flight lieutenant into a chair. He sat heavily and smiled wanly at Jacob. 'Hello,' he said, his voice strained with pain.

Jacob looked at the airman, then repeated, 'Going down the line?'

'There is a network to aid crashed RAF personnel to escape from occupied Europe,' Madame Aubry explained. 'That is all you must know.'

'His next destination,' Mercator said, 'is a safe house twelve kilometres away. He must be guided there but the Germans are on tenterhooks after the café shooting. We cannot send a man with him, but,' Mercator added, looking straight at Jacob, 'we could an invisible French boy . . .'

Mercator needed to say nothing else. Jacob knew what was being demanded of him. 'Do I get a code name?' he asked.

Mercator thought for a moment and grinned. 'Yes,' he said. 'You're Nuisance.'

As they made their way along the road, the airman walking painfully with the aid of a stick, Jacob recited over and over again in his head a phrase Mercator had made him learn – *Mon oncle est bu, mon oncle est bu*. To aid the deception that Bax was a drunkard, the moth-eaten coat provided to replace his flying jacket had been liberally sprinkled with cognac.

The air was chilly. It had not been long after dawn that he and the airman had left La Tour, passed through the silent houses of Belmont and, instead of turning right for the town, had gone left, taking the road that followed the river upstream. A light mist rose off the water to drift like the ghosts of disembodied souls through the willows lining the banks.

It was slow going. The gash on Bax's head was not his only injury. He had also torn a ligament in his leg and suffered a deep cut in his thigh which Madame Aubry had tightly bound with strips of material, both to staunch the bleeding and to hold the wound closed. To make matters worse, the only pair of trousers that could be found to replace those of his uniform were a size too small and chafed at his flesh which was badly bruised. Every half-kilometre he had to rest for a few minutes.

By seven o'clock they had covered barely five kilometres. Jacob grew increasingly apprehensive. They began to meet more and more people on their way to work. Several farmhands cycled by, nodding a passing greeting. Jacob nodded back but said nothing. A man with a horse and cart stopped to ask if he might offer them a lift. As instructed by Mercator, Bax pretended not to hear and swayed about a bit, muttering incoherently. Jacob muttered Mercator's phrase in the most convincing French accent he could manage. The man grunted, '*l'ivrogne*', dismissed the pair of them with a flick of his hand, tapped the horse on the rump with his whip and drove off.

Shortly after eight o'clock Bax suddenly collapsed on a grassy bank beneath an almond tree and, dropping his stick, sunk his face in his hands.

'What's the matter?' Jacob whispered, standing next to him.

'I can't go on,' the airman murmured. 'My leg . . .'

There was a dark patch in the material of Bax's trousers. Jacob sat down next to him, at the same time keeping a wary eye out. A man and a boy sitting by the roadside invited attention.

'We can't stop,' Jacob said urgently.

In his head, Jacob ran over the list of landmarks Mercator had given him to find the route to the safe house. It had been too risky to put them on paper, never mind draw a sketch map. If they were stopped and searched, a little boy and his sozzled uncle might have got away with having no identity papers but, if they had a map on them, that would have meant curtains — as Mercator had bluntly put it.

'We're over halfway there,' Jacob added.

Bax just groaned. Jacob looked at the patch on his trousers. He did not need to touch it to know it was blood, that the walking must have opened up the wound in his calf, despite Madame Aubry's ministrations.

'Come on,' Jacob urged, standing up and hoping the airman would follow suit.

'You go on,' Bax moaned. 'I'll stay here. There'll be a Jerry patrol along. I'll surrender . . .'

Jacob had anticipated many problems on this walk, but Bax giving up on him had not been one of them. For a moment he was at a complete loss.

'You can't,' he pleaded.

Bax hunched forwards and stared at the dusty road.

'You can't,' Jacob said again, despair mounting in him. 'You just can't, because . . . because . . .' He searched for a good reason then found it — indeed, he thought of several. 'You can't because if you do, the Germans will see you've got French clothes on and they'll want to know who gave them to you and who helped you get to this road, and they'll make you tell them and then they'll find the others and arrest them, and they'll be taken to the Gestapo headquarters, and the guards will beat them to make them talk, and . . .'

He fell silent. The horror of the situation dawned upon him. This was, in all probability, what was happening to his mother. The realization, while it turned his stomach with fear, immediately put everything into perspective. It was as if, until now, it really had all seemed to him some kind of game, some thrilling adventure, although it was serious. Yet now it was not. It was a matter of life and death: his mother's, his, and that of this airman who was nearing the end of his ability to endure pain and hopelessness.

'Did they tell you my mother's being held by the Gestapo?' Jacob went on, his voice low, his eyes continually glancing up and down the road. 'That's why I came to France. I stowed away on a Lysander from our local airfield. Didn't you think it odd that an English boy was with the Resistance?'

Bax did not reply. He tentatively touched the patch of blood.

'You've got to go on,' Jacob said insistently. 'If you surrender the Germans will have won. And,' he added pointedly, 'if your friends knew, they'd think you were a coward not to at least try.'

'I have tried,' Bax muttered through gritted teeth.

'Well, try harder,' Jacob retorted. 'There's a lot of people have put themselves at great risk to help you.'

He stood up and set off slowly along the road. The situation seemed suddenly ridiculous, reminding him of a time he had refused to go with his mother to a barber's shop to have his hair cut. She had left him standing in the street, playing upon his insecurity to follow her. And he had.

Behind, he heard a shuffling sound. Bax had struggled to his feet and was making the effort to walk. Jacob retraced his steps.

'We'll get you down the line,' Jacob said encouragingly. 'If we keep our wits about us.'

A kilometre further on, they had to cross the river by

a narrow stone bridge. Hundreds of years old, it could accommodate a horse and rider, or someone with a hand cart, but not a motor vehicle. For this reason the Germans rarely bothered to guard it. Consequently, Resistance fighters quite often used it.

Stopping a hundred metres short of the bridge, Jacob left Bax in the shelter of a weeping willow and crept ahead through bushes to see how the land lay. What he saw first made his heart sink. Parked on the road at the beginning of the bridge was a German military motor-cycle and sidecar upon which was mounted a heavy machine gun. Standing in the centre of the bridge were two German soldiers, one armed with a rifle, the other with a sub-machine gun.

Worming his way back through the undergrowth to Bax, Jacob explained the situation. 'Now remember,' he finished, 'you're supposed to be drunk.'

Bax nodded, rose unsteadily to his feet and they set off towards the Germans, Jacob leading the airman by the hand. As they passed the motorbike and sidecar and started to cross the bridge, Bax began to hum tunelessly, leaning on his stick, pretending to lose his balance then regaining it. Jacob realized the act must have been excruciatingly painful.

The two Germans watched them approach impassively, stepping aside as if to let them pass. Yet at the last moment, the one with the rifle stuck his hand out.

'*Halt! Ausweis!*'

Jacob did not understand the command but he could guess what the soldier was demanding – identity papers.

'*Mon oncle est bu,*' Jacob said in what he hoped was a

credible French accent and with as much distress as he could manage.

'*Ausweis!*'

'*Mon oncle est bu,*' Jacob repeated tremulously. He pretended to cry, rubbing his eyes with one hand while tugging at Bax with the other. For his part, Bax swayed slightly, hummed three bars of the *Marseillaise* off-key and managed a convincing belch.

'*Ausweis!*'

At that moment came the ominous sound of the sub-machine gun being cocked.

'*Ausweis!*'

The guard was losing patience.

'*Mon oncle est bu,*' Jacob said yet again, hopelessly.

Then, to his utter amazement, the Germans started laughing. One of them was pointing at the dark stain on Bax's trousers.

It was several seconds before Jacob realized what the joke was. *They think,* he said to himself, *Bax is so drunk he's peed himself.*

The Germans stepped aside to let them through. At that moment, Jacob glanced up at his supposed uncle. A button on the airman's shirt had come open. Dangling in full view was his RAF identity disc, tied round his neck on a piece of cord.

Jacob gave Bax's hand a sharp wrench. The airman tripped, stumbled clumsily forwards past the Germans and fell against the bridge parapet. His stick went over the edge into the river. Jacob struggled to help him up. The Germans guffawed with laughter. Pulling Bax's arm round his shoulder, Jacob half-dragged him off the bridge and down the lane on the other bank.

For another hour and three-quarters, Jacob supported Bax. Now it was Jacob's turn to take a break every half-kilometre. The airman was heavy and, on a few occasions, almost lost consciousness. Most of the time he struggled on as if in a semi-trance, his jaw set and his eyes glazed with exhaustion and pain.

Eventually, the late morning sun hot on their faces, they arrived at the safe house, an isolated farmhouse surrounded on three sides by woods. Jacob knocked on the door. A muffled voice responded.

'*Je suis Nuisance,*' he declared, with not a little pride.

The door was unbolted and a young woman with permed hair, wearing a floral print dress, appeared.

'*Bonjour, Nuisance.*'

She ushered them in to a dark sitting room. The shutters were closed, the furniture old-fashioned and well past its best. It smelt like Jacob's grandparents' house. For a brief second he felt homesick, but suppressed it. There was no time for emotion. For Bax the day's journey was over but, for Jacob, it was only halfway through. After eating a piece of soft cheese and an apple, and taking a long drink of water, he bade the airman farewell and set off on his return, having decided to wade across the river rather than risk crossing the bridge again.

Striding along in the sunlight, with birds singing in the hedgerows and taking dust baths in the road ahead of him, the tension of the morning lifted from him, Jacob concentrated his thoughts on just one subject – the coal cellar beneath the alley off Boulevard Descartes.

5

It was late in the afternoon before Jacob arrived back at La Tour. Wading the river had not been possible. Nowhere was it shallow enough and although the dark water seemed placid, when he threw a branch into it an unseen current promptly whisked it away. This, he knew from going fishing with his grandfather, meant there might be a dangerous undertow so swimming it was also out of the question. Instead he had made his way back towards Belmont on the opposite bank, keeping to the fields, water meadows and woods.

Although he was not to know it when he set off, Jacob's detour proved to be for the best. All afternoon, along the road on the opposite bank that he had taken that morning with Bax, German military vehicles kept up a steady traffic. He saw truckloads of soldiers, several staff cars and a number of motorcycle combinations speed by. At one point a platoon of soldiers in battledress marched past.

Nearing Belmont, Jacob left the fields and came out on to the road leading to the village bridge upon which, he noticed with dismay, guards were posted. He was wondering how he could get across without papers when he was approached by a young man carrying a shepherd's crook and with a nondescript dog at his heels. It was Emile. He signalled for Jacob to wait behind a low hedge and disappeared, to come back twenty minutes later with a flock of two dozen sheep. Beckoning to Jacob, they drove the sheep over the bridge together, the guards not bothering to ask for identity papers.

'You've done very well,' Mercator congratulated Jacob when he reached the tower. 'A boy doing a man's job.'

'How did Emile know I was on the other side of the bridge?' Jacob asked.

'Trees have eyes and walls have ears,' Mercator replied enigmatically. 'Now go on up to your room and have a rest. We've a busy night ahead.' He smiled, adding, 'I would imagine you've acquired a taste for this kind of work?'

'It was frightening at the narrow bridge,' Jacob admitted.

'Good,' said Mercator. 'If you aren't frightened, you get cocky. And cocky equals killed.'

Jacob went up to his room and lay on his bed. For an hour, he could not sleep. Not only was the adrenalin still flowing in him but he could not stop pondering on how he might gain an entry into the Gestapo building. The coal hole cover, he was certain, was the way in. Comparatively, that was the easy part. Once inside the building he would have to find a way to success-fully reach the top floor undiscovered, locate his mother and then get not only her out but also himself. The task seemed impossible.

Finally he drifted into a troubled doze, a fitful dream pestering him in which a flock of sheep suddenly threw off their fleeces and stood up to reveal they were German soldiers with wolves' faces.

It was almost dark when Jacob was awoken by Mercator gently shaking his shoulder. Behind him hovered a shadowy figure. Jacob sat up to see a girl of about his own age standing in the room. She wore black trousers and a dark, long-sleeved blouse. Her hair was cut short.

'This is Angelique,' Mercator declared.

'Hello, Nuisance,' she said.

Jacob was embarrassed. 'Nuisance is my code name,' he replied defensively.

'I like to call you Nuisance,' Angelique replied cheekily, in perfect English.

'Don't you have a code name?' Jacob retorted, somewhat peeved.

'Never you mind what that is,' Mercator interrupted him. 'You've been told before – the less you know the better. Tidy yourself up and come downstairs.'

When Jacob descended the stairs it was to find Mercator, Angelique and Emile seated at the table with a circular tin open before them.

'Sit down,' Mercator said, 'and listen carefully.'

He pushed the tin across the table. Jacob peered into it. The contents looked like the grease his grandfather used to lubricate his farm machinery.

'Do you know what this is?'

'It's axle grease,' Jacob replied.

'It might appear like it,' Mercator agreed, 'but it is, in fact, carborundum paste for polishing metal surfaces mixed with a little grease. Whatever machine this is put into will very quickly seize up.' He reached under the table to produce two objects like giant metal syringes with side-mounted levers. 'These are grease guns,' Mercator continued. 'German army grease guns, to be precise. Vehicle mechanics use them. On the end is a nozzle that exactly fits the grease nipples on the bearings on German army vehicles. Not far from here is a German army transport division barracks. It's well guarded, but there is a way in. The trouble is, only a small person can manage it.'

Mercator produced a piece of paper upon which there was a simple diagram drawn. He spread it out on the table. 'Two metres in from the main perimeter barbed wire fence is an electric fence consisting of five strands of bare cable thirty centimetres apart and carrying a high voltage current. Normally, the bottom wire is only twenty centimetres from the ground. However, there is one spot where the wire passes over a dip in the ground and is forty centimetres up. Emile knows where and will take you there. Your job is to get in under the live wire with these grease guns and pump carborundum grease into the axle bearings of every vehicle you can. You'll each have a tin of doctored grease. Keep going until you run out. Are you game, Nuisance?'

'Yes,' Jacob replied without hesitation, 'but I don't know what a grease nipple looks like.'

'I will show you,' Angelique said. 'It is very easy.'

Jacob stared at her.

'Angelique has done this before,' Mercator explained, 'usually with her sister Monique. Monique, however, has a bad cough . . .'

Madame Aubry entered the tower with a tray of

cheese, bread and a bottle of wine. Mercator uncorked the bottle, pouring a small amount into five glasses and handing them round. 'Vouvray this time,' he told Jacob and he raised his glass. '*A votre santé!*'

Everyone raised their glass and drank. Jacob sipped at his wine. It had a dry, crisp aftertaste.

'What do you think of it?' Mercator enquired.

Jacob considered his response for a moment then said, 'It has a sort of taste of oak wood and apples.'

'Very astute. Do you like it?'

'Yes,' Jacob replied with an air of certainty.

'That's the best you can get,' Mercator stated with the authority of an expert. 'It's called the Huet Vouvray 'Le Haut Lieu' Moelleux of 1921. The Germans have drunk or confiscated all the stocks they can get their hands on but, if you know where to go . . .'

'"Oak wood and apples!"' Madame Aubry exclaimed. 'Such a discerning palate! We will make a connoisseur out of you before you leave France.'

As Emile put the tins of carborundum paste into two small knapsacks, Angelique showed Jacob how to reload a grease gun. When she was done, Mercator spoke again.

'It is important you don't leave any sign of your presence behind,' he said. 'The Germans must not know you've been there. If they suspect you've tampered with the vehicles they'll smell a rat and investigate. Now, off you go and –' he nodded at Jacob '– make a nuisance of yourselves.'

They set off on three bicycles, following Emile along field paths and narrow, little-used lanes with grass growing down the centre of them. It was not until well after midnight that they reached their destination, dismounting and hiding the bicycles under a dense bush.

The perimeter fence to the compound was in darkness. High overhead, the drone of heavy bombers explained why: there was an air raid blackout in force. A light ground mist hung in the air like smoke from a dying fire.

Emile guided them along a ditch that ended at the barbed-wire fence. Beyond that point it had been filled in but the soil had settled, providing the necessary gap. Very carefully he eased the bottom strand of barbed wire upwards with a short steel rod with a Y cut in one end. In the matter of a few seconds Angelique was under it. Jacob crawled after her, pulling himself along on his elbows. The electric fence looked innocuous yet, as Jacob started to crawl under it, he could hear it faintly buzzing. From an insulator on a nearby pole, a tiny spark intermittently danced, earthing itself through the mist. The sight of it reinforced in him the danger of what they were doing – and the proximity of being fried on a wire.

Ahead in the darkness, like the dense ghostly outlines of prehistoric beasts, stood row upon row of vehicles – trucks, half-track personnel carriers, staff cars, motorcycles, fuel tanker lorries . . .

Angelique beckoned. At a crouch, she moved slowly across the parking area to a huge truck on which was mounted an anti-aircraft spotlight. Jacob, checking there were no sentries in sight, joined her. She removed her grease gun from her knapsack and, raising the nozzle, pressed it against a small metal valve screwed into the rear axle bearing of the right wheel. Giving four short pumps on the grease gun lever, she twisted it free and moved to the left wheel, repeating the action.

'You understand?' she whispered, her lips close to his ear. Jacob nodded. 'Four pumps for big wheels, two for little,' she added. 'Ignore the motorcycles.' She pointed at the next row of stationary vehicles. 'You do that line. I meet you at the end.'

Jacob wriggled under the first vehicle, a staff car. Although it was the dead of a misty night and the military base was in darkness, there was sufficient starlight by which to see and, Jacob's eyes being accustomed to the night, he easily located the first grease nipple and injected two squirts of the carborundum paste. It took fifteen minutes to sabotage the bearings of the twenty-eight vehicles in the row.

When he finished the last, he found Angelique already waiting for him. She indicated he do the next row and she a line of parked half-tracks. They set off again.

It seemed so easy. Jacob found it hard to believe that just a few pumps of the grease gun would immobilize a huge lorry. Halfway down the row, the grease gun became empty. He removed the tin from his knapsack and reloaded the gun. His fingers became sticky with the grease and he wiped them on a square of cloth put in the knapsack for the purpose.

No sooner had Jacob replaced the tin in his knapsack than – with an abruptness that made him jump – the vehicle depot lights came on. He stayed quite still. At any moment he expected to hear the rasp of military boots on the concrete parking area. Yet all remained silent.

The lights being on slowed his progress from vehicle to vehicle. He could also now see beneath other vehicles the occasional shadowy movement that was Angelique.

Meeting up again, Angelique suggested they concentrate on two lines of heavier vehicles. After those, she suggested, they would be out of carborundum paste. Jacob agreed and they started off again.

By chance, every vehicle in Jacob's row was a heavy lorry, some mounted with anti-aircraft guns. Moving beneath them was comparatively easy going for they had a high ground clearance.

He was four vehicles down the line, lying beneath the rear axle of a six-wheeled truck, when he heard a snuffling noise. Glancing to one side, he noticed with alarm that a pair of human legs were walking slowly along the space between his row and Angelique's. Worse, it was accompanied by two pairs of canine ones. Both were moving with an animal-like stealth. Jacob cursed himself. It had not occurred to him that the sentries might wear rubber-soled boots. Or that there would be guard dogs.

The three pairs of legs drew level with him. Jacob held his breath in trepidation. The sentry's boots were so close he could, between the two right rear wheels of the truck, see the stitching in the leather.

Dog and sentry stopped. The latter's quiet voice issued a softly spoken command in German to the former. Jacob's heart missed a beat. The dog – Jacob could now see it was a large grey Alsatian – was sniffing at the wheels behind which he was lying. At any moment it would smell him.

Yet the dog made no indication of having located his presence. It was then Jacob realized that the strong odours of diesel fuel, grease, oil and metal were disguising the scent of his body. All he had to do was lie perfectly still.

The dog, however, did not move away. It continued to sniff at the wheels. Then, without warning, it cocked its leg. Warm canine urine splashed against the tyre, through the wheel spokes, on to the concrete, over Jacob's clothes and into his face. He screwed his lips tight, but not quickly enough. A bitter, salty taste stuck to his tongue. He wanted to gag but fought it.

As quietly as they had come, sentry and dog moved away. Jacob tried to rinse his mouth out with saliva. In vain.

Crawling back under the perimeter wire, Jacob went first but, on the way back to La Tour, Emile and Angelique insisted on riding in front of him. The moment he walked into the tower, Mercator wrinkled his nose. 'What, may I ask, is that noxious odour?' he enquired.

'It's me,' Jacob admitted, somewhat crestfallen.

Emile, who had seen the whole episode from the cover of the ditch, said, '*Un chien de garde a uriné . . .*' Then he collapsed into a fit of laughter.

Stifling a grin, Mercator said, 'Now you know what it's like to be a lamp post.'

'It's not funny,' Jacob sulked.

'Look at it this way,' Mercator added, 'better a German dog's water than a German soldier's bullet.'

For an hour, until well after first light, Jacob lay in Madame Aubry's bath tub. It took three latherings of his hair with her lavender scented shampoo to get the stink out. Even after cleaning his teeth twice, gargling with mouthwash and drinking a large mug of warm milk laced with brandy, he still fancied he tasted the dog in his throat.

He was just about to leave the bath and dry himself when the door opened and Angelique entered without knocking. She was carrying a pile of fresh clothes. Jacob instantly tried to cover himself with Madame Aubry's bath sponge.

'Don't worry,' Angelique remarked dismissively. 'I have brothers.' She sat on a stool by the basin stand, placing the clothes next to the water jug.

'I'd like to get out of the bath,' Jacob announced.

'Of course, but first I must tell you something. Half an hour ago, the staff car of *SS-Gruppenführer* von Giessler, the commander of the *Waffen-SS* in this region, left the German barracks. It – how do you say it in English? – conked out within ten kilometres.' She smirked broadly. 'So it was worth it?'

Jacob thought for a moment then replied, 'Yes. It was worth it. Now can I get out? The water's beginning to freeze.'

After his bath Jacob returned to La Tour and went to bed, sleeping deeply and not waking until the early afternoon. Going outside, he discovered Mercator sitting in a deckchair looking out over the orchard. He was in his shirtsleeves with his trouser legs rolled up and a pipe in his mouth. Under different circumstances, Jacob thought, he might just have been a retired bank manager on holiday.

'Good zizz?' Mercator asked as Jacob came up to him.

'Yes, thank you,' Jacob replied. 'I was more tired than I realized.'

'Excitement's a great sleeping potion,' Mercator observed.

Jacob sat down on the remains of one of the ruined chateau walls. The stones were almost too hot to touch. Butterflies danced and crickets sawed in the grass of the orchard.

'Can I ask you a question?' Jacob ventured at length.

'So long as you don't necessarily expect an answer,' Mercator said.

'Before the war, what did you do for a job?'

'What do you think I did?' Mercator rejoined.

'I don't know,' Jacob answered in all truthfulness. 'Were you a doctor or a lawyer or something like that?'

'I was a teacher,' Mercator divulged.

'What did you teach?'

'French and German. And, to the senior boys, Latin.'

'Where?'

'That would be telling,' Mercator said. 'But it was in England, in a quite famous school.'

'You mean, like Eton?' Jacob probed.

Mercator just smiled conspiratorially and said, 'Perhaps. Something like that.'

'Aren't you ever afraid?' Jacob enquired, turning the conversation.

Mercator removed his pipe and studied the tobacco in the bowl. It had gone out. He reached under the deckchair and, taking a tobacco pouch from the grass beneath it started to refill the bowl of his pipe, pushing the tobacco in with the blunt end of a small, silver-plated smoker's penknife.

'After facing the rabble of boys in the Fourth Remove, nothing could hold any fear in this world,' he replied, but then he stopped refilling his pipe. 'Yes, Jacob,' he allowed in a soft, almost meditative, voice. 'I'm afraid all the time. Even when I'm asleep, I'm afraid.'

'Even now?'

'Even now, when I know there isn't a German within five kilometres and Pierre is tucked up in the grass down at the bottom of the orchard with his Sten in his lap watching the village.'

He carried on lighting his pipe. The tobacco smoke was dark blue as it rose in the sunlight and heavily perfumed. Jacob let him puff on it for a minute before speaking again.

'Is there any news of my mother?'

Mercator considered his reply.

'She is still being held at Boulevard Descartes. According to our information the Germans plan to move her tomorrow afternoon by road to Paris. There she will be kept at the Gestapo headquarters on the Avenue Foch.'

'Are we going to rescue her? I think I know a way into the building. There's a coal hole in the alley. I'm sure I could squeeze through it. It can't be any smaller than the gap under the electric fence . . .'

'That won't be possible, Jacob,' Mercator said.

'If I was to create a diversion . . .'

Mercator made no response.

'Can't we ambush the car they take her to Paris in?' Jacob suggested eagerly.

'No, Jacob. We cannot,' Mercator answered after a pause.

'But you must!' Jacob exclaimed in desperation.

There had to be something Mercator – or his group –

could do. They could surely not just stand by and let his mother be taken away.

'It's too risky,' Mercator said, gazing into the distance. 'It would take at least ten men to hold up the vehicle and the motorcycle outriders that will be sure to accompany it. There would be an exchange of fire and we can't afford the possible loss of life. Besides, we need every man we've got tomorrow for a big daylight attack.' He turned to face Jacob. 'I'm so sorry, Jacob. That's just the way it is.'

Jacob was determined not to cry and bit the inside of his lip hard to stop the tears from coming.

'There's something else,' Mercator continued. 'We've had a radio message from London. There's a Lysander coming in tomorrow night. You're going back on it.'

6

Leaving Mercator smoking his pipe, Jacob went into the tower and up to the top floor where he sat in one of the windows, hugging his knees. Below, the French countryside was spread out before him, the village of Belmont resting in the flat glare of the afternoon sunlight.

Mercator's announcement greatly disturbed Jacob. He had not expected a Lysander to come so soon. Worse, he now knew that to rescue his mother was a virtually impossible task.

If, Jacob considered, the coal hole could be opened, he was certain he would be able to lower himself through it into the cellar beneath. However, even if he could gain access to the Gestapo building, he would still not be able to get his mother out of it on his own, and Mercator was not going to sanction a rescue attempt.

His hopes had been shattered, his coming to France had been a complete waste of time. Every risk he had taken had not paid off.

He had, Jacob thought, got so near. He had stood in the street outside the very building in which his mother was incarcerated. He had looked up and seen the dormer windows behind one of which she was almost certainly being kept prisoner. Indeed, he had been so close that, had he called out, his mother would probably have heard him.

It then came to him that he would never see his mother again. The Germans would not let her go: they would, eventually, kill her.

Very quietly, Jacob began to sob, the tears running down his cheeks, falling to his knees and soaking into his trousers.

For ten minutes, Jacob cried and then he stopped. This was not, he told himself, what either of his parents would have expected of him. His father would have told him to stop blubbing and get a grip. His mother would have put her arm round him and said, consolingly – he could almost hear her voice now – '*Tears don't water the flowers.*' They had been, he remembered, the last words she had spoken to him.

Wiping his cheeks, he sat and pondered the situation, breaking it into its component parts as he might one of Stodgy's algebraic problems. First: his mother was being moved tomorrow and he was going to be returned to England that night, so whatever he did would have to be done in the morning. Second: he thought he could get into the building and he was told his mother was on the top floor, so her whereabouts should not be too difficult to locate. Third: no one else would help him because they were going to be involved in a raid. Fourth . . . There was no fourth.

Jacob's next move was to find Stodgy's common denominator that would start to bring the puzzle together. Yet, try as he might, he could see no way any one of the three facets of the problem could tie in with another. Each was separate, unique and unconnected.

Finally he resigned himself to defeat, his spirits crushed. All he would be able to say was that he had done his best, his best had not been good enough, and he had failed.

That evening, as Jacob remained disconsolate in the window, a dilapidated Renault flat-bed truck piled high with hay drove up. The moment it halted, a small wiry man climbed out of the back, brushing hay stalks off his clothing and sneezing once, violently. At the same time, Mercator removed a steel case the size of a small suitcase from under the hay and slapped his hand on the wooden tailboard. The gearbox screeched and the Renault immediately departed in a drift of filthy black fumes and dust.

Soon after, Jacob heard footsteps coming up through the tower and Mercator entered the room, followed by the man.

'Jacob, this is Grocer,' Mercator introduced him.

'So this is the famous Nuisance,' the man observed. 'I've heard about you in radio traffic with London. Useful with a grease gun, too, I understand.'

He walked across to Jacob, his hand extended. Jacob shook it and said, 'How do you do, sir.'

'I do very well,' Grocer replied.

'Grocer is here to help us with tomorrow's raid,' Mercator explained.

'One in which we wondered if you would take an important part,' Grocer added. 'A farewell snub at the Nazis before you return.'

'What would I be doing?' Jacob enquired.

'Come downstairs and we'll brief you with the others.'

In the main room on the ground floor were gathered Emile, André who had met the Lysander, Madame Aubry, Pierre from the café and Angelique.

'*Nous parlerons en Anglais pour Jacob,*' Mercator began, pronouncing Jacob's name as Yacob. '*D'accord?*'

'*Oui, d'accord,*' the others replied.

'Good,' Mercator declared. 'Now to business. Our target tomorrow is the fuel depot in the yard behind the Gestapo and general command building in Boulevard Descartes. As those of you who have reconnoitred it will know, there is a considerable amount of petrol and diesel stored there, in underground and above-ground tanks, fuel delivery vehicles and barrels. In addition, there is some aviation kerosene and, André thinks, about fifty thousand rounds of assorted ammunition, most of it small arms. What we hope to do is to blow the lot.'

There was an exchange of glances and broad grins.

'*Très bien!*' Emile exclaimed.

'It will be good,' Pierre remarked.

'The plan is this. André has discovered, running under the area, a number of drains. Built about one hundred and fifty years ago, they are not sewers but storm drains, put in to stop the town flooding when the river rose. There are three vents to these drains, covered by heavy metal grilles sunk deep into the surrounding stone frame. There is no way we can lift these. However, this doesn't matter. We can gain access to them through a narrow culvert in Rue Voltaire. It's little more than a slit but . . .' Mercator looked at Jacob and Angelique '. . . you two thin little creatures could slip through as easily as swallowing an oyster.'

Jacob tried to imagine what swallowing an oyster might be like and decided it would not be pleasant. Nevertheless, he got the gist of Mercator's metaphor.

Grocer took up the briefing. 'Once inside, you two head along the tunnels. Nothing to be afraid of. We'll give you each a torch. You'll have to walk about a hundred and fifty metres to the metal grilles. These are reached from the tunnel floor by means of metal rungs set in the stone walls. You shouldn't have to climb more than about three metres. Got it so far?' He did not wait for Jacob and Angelique to answer; he took it for granted. 'The rest of us will be outside the fuel depot. If anything untoward happens, we'll put down covering fire to give you a chance to withdraw. That said, I don't think the Germans will have an inkling of your presence if you keep quiet and go about your task silently.'

'What task?' Jacob enquired.

Emile placed on the table the box Jacob had seen Mercator take from the hay lorry. It had metal catches which he snapped open, lifting off the lid. Grocer removed a package about the size of a building brick, wrapped in brown greaseproof paper.

'This is PE,' he said.

'PE?' Jacob repeated. The only PE he knew was Physical Exercise, period 4, Monday mornings in the school playground, come rain or shine.

'Plastic explosive,' Mercator explained. 'It was

invented just before the war and is made of cyclonite, also known as hexogen or RDX. It is more powerful than any other known explosive, highly malleable and very versatile.'

Grocer put the wrapping aside. In his hand was a block of what looked, to Jacob, like a cross between his grandmother's butter and putty.

'Your task,' Grocer continued, 'is to place charges of PE around the metal grilles and up the sides of the vertical shafts leading to them.'

Jacob felt his face draining of blood. It was one thing to sabotage a line of vehicles, quite another to blow up an entire fuel store. As for handling explosives, he had on occasion touched his grandfather's shotgun cartridges but this – this was something altogether different and, he was more than aware, highly dangerous.

'I know what's on your mind,' Grocer said, cutting into Jacob's thoughts. 'You've nothing to worry about.'

Grocer tore off a corner of the explosive block. It came away in his hand like dense bread dough. Rolling it quickly into a ball, he threw it at the wall. Jacob instinctively flinched. The explosive hit the plaster with a dull thump and fell to the floor. Emile leaned over in his chair, picked it up and handed it to Grocer who stuck it back on the block.

'Perfectly safe,' Grocer announced. 'This is not like gelignite or dynamite or nitroglycerine, that you only have to shake to blow yourself into the middle of next month. This will not go off without a time fuse and a detonator stuck deep inside it.' He put his hand back in the box. 'And these,' he held them out for all to see, 'are the fuse and detonator.'

Jacob looked at them. About the size and thickness of a propelling pencil, the fuse consisted of a thin metal tube fashioned in two parts, one of aluminium and the other of copper, with three holes in the top and a coloured strip painted red wrapped around the middle hole. Above the holes was a perforated section painted black. The detonator looked like a length of thick cord about six centimetres long.

'This is what you do,' Grocer explained. 'You insert the end of the detonating cord in the black section of the pencil. This you then wrap round with a good thickness of PE, with the pencil sticking out. That I won't do. There's enough PE in this block to reduce this tower and Madam's cottage next door into a crater in the ground a metre deep. Then, you remove this little coloured strip and you squeeze the copper end of the fuse. Just pinch it. That's all. Put a dent in the side. Then,' he finished, 'you get the hell out of it. The red strip means you've got about nineteen minutes before the whole lot goes skywards.'

'What actually happens?' Jacob asked. 'In the fuse, I mean.'

'When you squeeze the copper section, you break a little glass ampoule inside that contains acid. This eats through a thick wire that holds a spring shut. When the wire breaks, the spring is released and drives a pointed striker against a tiny explosive charge just inside the top. This goes off and causes the detonating cord to explode. This, in turn, sets off the PE.'

'I think,' Mercator suggested, 'we might give this a go. We've twenty fuses so we can afford to waste one or two.'

'Agreed,' Grocer replied and, taking two fuses, led everyone outside.

It was now dusk, bats flying round the tower with a night bird Jacob could not identify plaintively calling some way off in the direction of the path. Grocer handed Jacob and Angelique a fuse each.

'Take off the coloured ring. Hold the fuse by the aluminium section. Grasp the copper section and gently bend it.'

They did as they were ordered. Jacob felt something break inside the fuse.

'Put your fuses down on the ground by the ruined wall and come back here.'

They obeyed.

'Now we go inside and wait.'

Once back in the tower, Grocer cut the block of explosive in two. Giving Jacob one half and Angelique the other, he continued with the instruction.

'The rest is a piece of cake,' he declared. 'You take the PE to the metal grille and, rolling it out into a sausage about the thickness of your wrist, you stick it all round the metal frame. From one point, you stick a sausage downwards on the wall to the bottom. In the base of that, you insert the detonating cord and time fuse. Now, let's try rolling out some PE.'

For quarter of an hour, Jacob and Angelique rolled the plastic explosive between their palms, practised sticking it to the wall and watched as Grocer showed them how to insert the detonating cord.

'Right!' Grocer announced as he shaped the explosive back into a block and wrapped it up, putting it in the box. 'Got the idea?

Jacob and Angelique exchanged glances and nodded.

'Grand stuff!' Grocer said and he looked at his watch. 'Any minute now . . .'

A few moments later, there came from outside two sharp reports, like fireworks going off. They were twenty seconds apart.

'Time for bed, I think,' Mercator said. 'We've all of us a long but, hopefully, fruitful day ahead of us tomorrow.'

It was a warm night. Jacob lay on his bed, the blanket and sheet piled in a heap on the floor, the window open. In the room below, the others were sleeping, with the exception of Angelique who had gone to Madame Aubry's cottage, and Emile who was ordered to keep the first two hours' lookout duty. Jacob could hear him moving stealthily around outside.

He could not sleep. Twenty-four hours from now, he thought, he would be back at Shawcross Farm and his mother would be in Paris. After that . . . He dared not consider the future.

Shortly after midnight, he heard low voices outside his window. Going to the sill and looking down, he could just make out André relieving Emile from his duty. The latch on the door to the tower clicked open and then shut.

Once again, not because he hoped for success but because he felt he had to, Jacob ran over in his mind the elements of his dilemma except that, this time, he put them in a different sequence. As far as his mother's rescue was concerned, he was on his own. His mother was in the Gestapo building, on the top floor. He had to make his move in the morning. His mother was to be taken to Paris in the afternoon. In the morning, he was to plant the explosives for the raid. He was leaving France the following night. The fuel depot was behind the Gestapo building. The coal cellar was accessible by way of the coal hole. The raid would cause chaos . . .

Jacob's thoughts suddenly stopped. There was a new element to the problem now, another aspect to be factored in which had not existed in the afternoon.

It was, Jacob considered, just like the solving of a mathematical equation. One just had to worry it, shake it about a bit, kick it into play and shape it into a rational order.

He looked out of the window at the orchard and the roofs of Belmont. Quite calmly, Jacob went over his plan in his mind, several times, trying to assess where its weaknesses lay. After ten minutes he gave up. If every risk in what he was intending to do were a hole, he pondered, his plan would look like a string vest that the moths had had a go at – but it was all he had. And as his father used to say on Grand National day, the only occasion in the year when he placed a bet on a horse, it might be an outsider but he considered it was worth a punt.

7

Since the shooting at the café, the Germans had tightened their grip on the town. Patrols roamed the streets, arresting anyone whom they thought even passingly suspicious. Roadblocks were set up on every road leading into the town. Not only motor vehicles were stopped; so, too, were carts and bicycles. Even farmers with wheelbarrows had them up-ended, their produce kicked or trampled underfoot. Pedestrians and elderly women carrying shopping bags were searched, roughly manhandled against a nearby wall and prodded with rifle barrels. If they were carrying food, the Germans confiscated or ruined it.

André, Angelique and Mercator entered the town through the roadblocks. Their papers were in order and they aroused no suspicion. Grocer, whose identity papers were not local, and Jacob – who had none at all – approached by way of a ditch which started about a kilometre from the periphery of the town and meandered between fields towards a large abandoned house on the outskirts, the owners of which had been arrested by the Nazis over a year before.

Once in the safety of the grounds, which were overgrown and unkempt, they waited until Emile and Pierre arrived, following their route along the ditch and carrying the weapons and explosives between them. Not long afterwards, one by one, the others rendezvoused with them in a thicket of rhododendron bushes next to what must have once been an ornamental pond but was now just a pool of stagnant water surrounded by water lilies gone to seed.

Jacob and Angelique were each given four blocks of PE with six fuses and six lengths of detonating cord. These were hidden in cotton bags, suspended by a thick string round their necks to hang inside their shirts. The fuses were all colour-coded red, giving approximately a nineteen-minute delay.

As three people together could raise German suspicion, it was decided André would lead Jacob and Angelique to Rue Voltaire, walking a hundred metres ahead of them. They were to follow, holding hands like brother and sister. The more innocent their appearance the less likely they were to be stopped.

By nine o'clock, they were ready.

'Remember,' Grocer said. 'Get back to the culvert as quickly as possible. When the charges go off, a blast wave'll travel along the drain faster than a horse can gallop. If you get caught in that, the pressure of the air alone will probably kill you, never mind the heat. When you get out, do exactly as you are told by André. All understood?'

'Yes,' Jacob and Angelique confirmed in unison.

'Good luck.'

They set off. It took twenty minutes to reach Rue

Voltaire. On the way, André was accosted by two German policemen. While they questioned him and studied his identity documents, Jacob and Angelique walked on by unmolested, waiting round the next corner for their guide to catch them up. Once in Rue Voltaire, they discovered Emile lingering by the entrance to a narrow passageway leading to a yard behind a disused warehouse. A painted sign, faded by the sun, read *M. Busson et Fils – Marchands de Mais.*

'*Voici le tunnel,*' Emile said, nodding towards the passageway.

The culvert was tucked in under a stone wall a few metres down the passageway.

With André and Emile keeping watch, Angelique and Jacob slipped through it. Beyond the opening was a steep slope down which they almost rolled. Jacob wondered how they were going to get back up it but put this concern from his mind. Better, he thought, to face obstacles one at a time.

Not talking for fear that the sound of their voices might travel along the tunnel, they switched on their torches and shone them around.

The storm drain was a wide circular tunnel at least two metres high, lined with ancient bricks. From the ceiling hung tendrils of roots. Here and there, water dripped from above to form puddles. The air was motionless, chilled and smelt musty. Jacob had expected the drain to be filthy, alive with rats or cockroaches and strewn with rubbish but, except for the puddles, some soil, dead roots and a few fallen bricks where a section was starting to cave in, it was comparatively clean. Clearly, Jacob thought, it must be periodically sluiced out by the river flooding.

Every twenty metres or so, side drains joined the main watercourse but this did not confuse either Jacob or Angelique. Most of these were small, insufficiently big for them to even crawl into, never mind walk. Several dribbled water over the bricks, leaving a pile of mud.

They had walked for about five minutes when, on turning a corner, a shaft of brilliant light illuminated the tunnel ahead. It was the first of the three grilles. They went past it and on to the second and third which were not much more than ten metres apart. Angelique signalled that she would do the third one and set off towards it, leaving Jacob to deal with the second.

Jacob switched off his torch and, unbuttoning his shirt, removed the two bags. They were heavy. The weight had made his neck ache. Squatting down just outside the circle of light, he unwrapped the first block of PE and, as quickly as he could, broke it into quarters. Yet before he started to shape it, he put one of the fuses and a short length of detonating cord in his trouser pocket.

Rolling the PE between his hands, Jacob hurriedly fashioned four sausages of the explosive, each about thirty centimetres long. Draping these over his shoulder, he looked up. The sunlight was so bright it hurt his eyes. The steps up to the grating were nothing more than hoops of rusty iron. Grabbing the first, and praying the hoops would bear his weight, he started to haul himself up.

If, Jacob thought, a German guard was to walk over

the grille now, and look down, he would see Jacob peering up at him. All he would then have to do is aim his rifle between the bars . . . He put the thought from his mind and, hooking one arm through the top hoop, set about pressing the PE around the sides of the grille. It adhered easily to the stone and metal.

He was just fixing the fourth sausage in place when his head was suddenly filled with a deep droning sound that seemed to echo up from the tunnel beneath. It increased in volume to almost the pitch of continuous thunder. The sunlight was instantaneously cut off. Glancing up, Jacob saw the underneath of a vehicle chassis pass overhead. Then the sunlight exploded upon him again.

The four sausages did not entirely surround the grille so Jacob climbed down to the tunnel, opened a second block of PE and made another followed by a much longer and thinner strip of explosive. Returning to the grille, he put the last sausage in place, joining the explosive into a circle. From that, he began to run the thinner strip downwards, pressing it into the stone but making sure there was no break in it. Back on the tunnel floor, he ended the strip with a thick wadge of PE in the middle of which he embedded the length of detonating cord. Finally, his hands shaking, he added the time fuse.

It was set.

Angelique appeared and gave Jacob a quizzical look, her eyebrows raised questioningly.

Jacob nodded and gave her the thumbs-up.

Together, they retreated to the first grille and, together, set the charges there. When they were finished, they still had a block of PE left over so Jacob climbed up to the grille and pressed it as one lump against the wall of the vertical shaft.

'Done!' he whispered as his feet touched the tunnel floor once more.

Angelique grinned and murmured, 'Now we . . .' and she mimed bending the end of the fuses.

Together they retraced their steps. As Angelique went on to her first charge, Jacob took the fuse for the second grille in his hands and, very slowly, bent the copper section. He felt the little glass vial of acid inside break. It was done, he thought. Nothing could undo it. He had started a course of action going that would, in less than twenty minutes, release a spring that would drive a plunger that would trigger a percussion cap that would set off the detonating cord that would cause a massive explosion. And kill men.

The enormity of what he had just done shocked him. Yet Jacob knew this was his duty. The men above were the enemy. And they were holding his mother captive.

Angelique touched Jacob on his sleeve. 'Now we go!' she whispered, switching her torch back on.

They ran to the third fuse, Jacob bent the end and they fled, running as quietly yet as quickly as they could, their feet splashing in the puddles and the beams of their torches dancing on the walls.

At the culvert, they stopped. The slope down which they had come was too steep to climb. Jacob tried running at it but he could get only halfway up.

'We're stuck here,' he said with alarm, recalling Grocer's terse warning of the blast wave and not bothering if anyone heard him or not. 'What do we do now?'

'*Pas de problème*,' Angelique remarked calmly and,

pursing her lips, she gave a short coo, like a mourning dove. A moment later a knotted rope snaked down the slope and a muffled voice from above said, urgently, '*Vite! Vite!*'

Angelique went first. When Jacob reached the top of the rope, two strong hands grabbed him by the shoulders and pulled him through the gap.

'*Allez au café de Pierre,*' André said. They handed him the torches, he let the rope drop down the culvert and they walked away in opposite directions.

Without obviously hurrying, Jacob and Angelique made their way to the main square. Some stalls had been set up under the trees, selling vegetables, eggs and poultry, cheese, fruit and other farm produce. Women moved between them, arguing over prices. Observing them from opposite ends of the square were two groups of German policemen, their weapons at the ready, their eyes roving over the shoppers, watching for anything even slightly suspicious. The café was doing a brisk trade, serving wine or coffee to the farmers and shoppers. Seated at one table was Mercator, a glass of white wine before him. Grocer was nowhere to be seen.

Angelique went straight to Mercator, kissed him on the cheek and said, '*Bonjour, Papa!*'

'*Bonjour, ma chérie!*' Mercator replied, returning her kiss and looking at Jacob. '*Bonjour, Jacques!*'

'*Bonjour, Papa,*' Jacob responded, taking Angelique's cue.

They sat down at the table.

'Pierre!' Mercator called, leaning backwards in his chair. '*Deux limonades, s'il vous plaît.*'

'*Oui, m'sieur,*' Pierre answered from within the café.

Jacob gazed around the square. It all looked so normal. Then he caught sight of Emile standing in the *pissoir*. Jacob could see he was only pretending to relieve himself.

Mercator glanced at his watch. Pierre reappeared carrying two glasses of lemonade on a tray. He reached the table and was about to put them down when there was a massive explosion, almost immediately followed by another. A fireball mushroomed into the sky behind the buildings across the square.

For a second, nothing else moved. Then there was pandemonium. A donkey in the traces of a farmer's cart took fright and sped off across the square, scattering artichokes and cabbages across the cobbles. Birds flew terrified from the trees. People began to run hither and thither, shouting. A tray of eggs splattered on to the ground. A barrel of wine that had fallen from a stall struck by the donkey, split open to flow down the gutter, sweeping leaves ahead of itself. The ground momentarily shook as if there had been an earthquake.

In that instant of initial panic, Jacob jumped to his feet and sprinted away from the café. Within seconds he was running as hard as he could down Rue Puget, heading for Boulevard Descartes. Behind him Jacob could hear Mercator calling him, but he ignored him.

When Jacob hurtled round the corner, the boulevard was teeming with German soldiers and policemen. The pavements were covered in shattered glass. Not a single window remained intact in any building. Under a tree, a German soldier was sitting in a daze, blood pouring down his face from a gash in his scalp. He kept trying to wipe it out of his eyes.

Slipping on the broken glass, Jacob headed straight for the Gestapo building. The Germans paid him no attention. They were busy tending to the injured. Officers barked out orders. Men in trim Gestapo uniforms came tumbling down the steps of the building. From several shattered windows fluttered a blizzard of sheets of paper. A pall of dense black smoke rose from behind it, folding in on itself, flickers of hellish flame dancing within it.

Suddenly there was another tremendous explosion. A cast-iron manhole in the boulevard ten metres from Jacob was hurled into the air, pirouetting like a bizarre tiddlywink. It crashed down on one of two military staff cars. The driver yelled with pain as the roof above him caved in. Then he was silent.

Debris started to shower down. Pieces of blazing wood began to fall all round Jacob. Jagged chunks of metal rattled on the road. The Germans took cover wherever they could.

Oblivious to the deadly hail, Jacob headed for the alley. The air within it was sweltering, blowing towards him like a wind out of the gates of hell. He reached the coal hole. The cover was still in place. Kneeling down on the ground, close into the wall for cover, Jacob tugged the length of detonating cord out of his pocket and pressed it into the gap round the rim of the iron disc. Thrusting the end of it into the time fuse, he looked round for something with which to hit it, not to break the acid reservoir but to smash the wire that held the internal spring. There was nothing.

'I can't wait twenty minutes for it to go off,' he said aloud to himself.

From over the wall of the compound there came another, more muffled explosion followed by the crackle of ammunition going off. Bullets started to zip into the alley, ricocheting off the walls and cobbles.

At that moment a Gestapo officer came running down the alley, pulling a Luger automatic pistol from a holster on his belt as he ran.

'*Halt!*' he yelled. '*Was zum Teufel machst du da?*'

Jacob turned. The officer was standing not three metres from him, the automatic pistol aimed at his head. He saw the officer's finger tighten on the trigger. Yet he did not fire. Instead he stood quite still for a moment then, buckling at his knees, pitched forward on to the cobbles. The Luger flew from his hand, rattling across the ground towards Jacob. The back of the man's head was missing. Another stray round struck sparks off the wall of the alley. Chips of stone spat at Jacob, stinging his cheeks.

Cautiously picking up the Luger, Jacob stepped back, crouched down and fired at the detonating cord. He missed. He fired again. The trigger was too stiff. He could not aim the weapon accurately.

As much in despair as anger, he hurled the gun at the dead Gestapo officer – and then he saw it. On the man's belt was a sheath with a dagger in it, the boss decorated with a swastika. Jacob ran at a crouch to the body and, unfastening the retaining strap, pulled the dagger free. The body gave a spasm but Jacob did not care. He returned to the coal hole, prised the cover up with the dagger, got his fingers under the rim and, heaving, pushed it aside. Beneath he could see the coal chute.

Without bothering to check if anyone was watching, he lowered himself through the hole.

The coal cellar gave on to a whitewashed corridor lined with boxes of stationery and a number of grey, metal filing cabinets. At the far end was a door. Jacob opened it cautiously to be faced with a flight of stone stairs at the top of which was another door, beside which more boxes of documents were stacked. This he also opened a few centimetres, only to shut it again very smartly. It was impossible for him to go that way. On the other side of the door was the main entrance hall to the building, bustling with German soldiers.

Jacob backtracked. At the foot of the stone stairs was another door. He opened it to find himself in an L-shaped room that must, he reasoned, have once been a butler's pantry. There was a porcelain sink with brass taps above it, a series of dusty shelves lined with empty bottles and jars and, high up against the ceiling, a board of bell indicators that would have summoned maids upstairs. Going round the angle in the room, Jacob came face to face with a second, wooden flight of steps. This, he guessed, was the servants' staircase.

He quickly ascended it, not bothering to keep silent. From outside, he could hear continuing intermittent explosions as more ammunition went off. The rest of the building was filled with the sound of running footsteps, shouted orders and confusion.

At the second floor, Jacob paused to look out of one of the tiny garret-like windows that were the only source of light in the stairwell. Beyond the immediate grounds of the house was the fuel depot. The fuel tanks had ruptured, pouring flaming diesel oil down into a crater at least twenty metres across, balancing on the rim of which was a blazing lorry, its tyres dripping molten burning rubber. Spreadeagled nearby, burning, was the body of the driver. Over everything hung a swelling, curling pall of jet black smoke.

On each floor a door gave on to the main staircase but Jacob waited until he reached the top before he chanced pushing one of them ajar.

Beyond the door was a carpeted landing upon which stood a desk, a chair and a telephone which, Jacob noticed, was off the hook. He could see three other doors. They were all shut. There was nobody in sight.

Stepping out on to the landing, Jacob took a deep breath and, in four paces, was at the first door. He put his hand on the knob and turned it. The room was an office. He closed it and moved to the next. That contained only a long table and some chairs, a bare light hanging from a ceiling rose. The third room contained two desks, a wall cupboard and, to one side, a long-range military radio set. It was switched on, a soft but high-pitched whine issuing from a pair of headphones hastily cast off to hang by their wires over the back of the operator's chair. By the message pad and Morse key was a half-drunk cup of coffee, steam still rising from it.

Of his mother, there was no sign.

A wave of despairing panic ran through Jacob. Mercator's informant had been wrong. Or lying. They had moved her already, he thought. He forced himself to concentrate, falling back on Stodgy's saying. He could hear the exhortation now: *AFT, boys! AFT!*

Jacob counted off the points on his fingers. There was no proof positive that his mother had been moved. Parked outside were two staff cars, whereas on his first visit there had been only one. Was the second for his mother? She was being held, as best he knew, on the top floor. But where? There were only these three rooms and she was not in any of them. Yet, as he went over these details, something niggled at the back of his mind. He was overlooking something . . .

There was another muffled explosion from the direction of the fuel depot. A hot breeze carried into the room through the broken window, dislodging a piece of glass which fell from the frame to shatter on the sill. It made Jacob jump.

In a split second, as if by divine revelation, it then came to him. The window was an ordinary casement. The top floor windows were dormers. He was *not* on the top floor.

Jacob went out on to the landing. There were no stairs leading upwards, no doors other than that through which he had come. The rooms contained only office furniture and the radio. What did one room have, he asked himself, that the other two lacked? It took only a few moments to realize the answer. It was the wall cupboard.

He opened it. On the other side was a tight spiral staircase going up. Jacob closed the door behind him and mounted it, step by step. Just as he was about to turn the last twist in the spiral, he heard someone cough.

Very gradually, Jacob raised his head above the top

step. Standing at one of the dormer windows looking out was a German policeman. He was so near, Jacob could make out quite distinctly the silver eagle and the letters *SD* on a badge on the arm of his jacket. He wore polished black boots, his trousers tucked into them, and a black belt with a holster on his left side. His steel helmet lay on a chair between two closed doors.

Acting almost on impulse, Jacob quickly climbed the last few steps. The policeman, intent on watching the chaos outside, did not see him. He walked past him then turned to face him.

'*Bonjour, m'sieur!*' he said, in a loud voice.

The policeman whirled round, stepping back from the window. He opened his mouth to speak, simultaneously reaching for his holster. At that point, Jacob ran at him with all his might, ramming his shoulder into the man's belly. The German lost his balance and fell backwards down the staircase. Jacob, grabbing the man's helmet by the chin strap, ran after him. The turn in the stairs had broken his fall. Jacob raised the helmet, ready to hit him over the head with it. The man was prone, lying on his back, not moving. From the grotesque angle of his head, Jacob could see his neck had snapped.

Dropping the helmet on the dead body, Jacob returned to the landing. He tried the first door. Inside he found a bed and an upright chair – nothing else. The second door was locked but on a hook to one side hung a key. His hand shaking, he inserted it in the keyhole. The oiled mechanism clicked. He opened it.

The room was small and, like the other, contained a bed and a chair. The dormer window was blown in, slivers of glass scattered across a threadbare square of carpet. Upon the bed was hunched a figure, lying on its side facing the wall. It was wearing a pair of dark grey trousers and a stained white shirt. Its hair was cut short like a man's, its feet bare and bruised.

Jacob hesitated then said softly, 'Mum?'

The figure did not move.

'Mum,' he said again, louder. 'It's Jacky.'

The figure stirred and turned over.

'*Je ne sais pas . . .*' it mumbled.

Tentatively, Jacob stepped forwards to get a closer look. The figure slowly sat up.

'Mum . . .?'

The figure looked up at him. It was his mother. She had a black eye. Her bottom lip had been cut, the blood now congealed into a large, dark scab. Across her forehead was a livid scar. Dried blood had drawn a line down her neck from her left ear.

'Jacob?' The voice was both tremulous and incredulous. 'Jacky?' it said again. 'My Jacky? How can you be . . .?'

His mother's speech was slurred. She was finding it hard to move her mouth.

'It's a long story,' Jacob replied. 'We've got to move fast. Can you stand up?'

'I think so.' His mother got to her feet, swaying slightly.

'I've come to rescue you,' Jacob announced firmly.

Until that moment Jacob had given no thought as to how he would physically get his mother out of the building. Just to discover her whereabouts had been enough. Yet, as he helped her out of the door, the answer came to him.

'Sit here,' he said, indicating the *SD* guard's chair.

As his mother did as she was told, Jacob went down the stairs to where the man was lying. As quickly as he could, he unbuttoned the corpse's jacket. This done, he undid its belt and trousers. The flesh was still warm and resilient. Jacob tried to think of the man as unconscious, not stone dead. The buttons open, he tugged off the boots followed by the trousers. Rolling the body on to its side, he stripped off the jacket. He baulked at removing the man's brown shirt but he did undo his tie. Gathering all the clothes up with the helmet, he took the stairs two at a time.

'Put these on,' he said. 'Quickly.'

He turned his back as his mother undressed and struggled into the uniform. 'Jacky, I can't do up the buttons.'

Jacob turned. His mother's hands were black and blue.

'They've broken some of my fingers,' she said, almost apologetically.

Jacob started to fasten the buttons up, embarrassed when he got to the trousers. His mother gave a brief giggle. Jacob looked up. Her face was not smiling but her eyes were.

'What's so funny?'

'You dressing me,' she answered. 'Not so long ago, I was dressing you.'

With the uniform on, Jacob held his mother steady as she pushed her feet into the boots. She grimaced with pain. Finally, he knotted the tie about her neck and put the helmet on her head, tightening the chin strap.

'Now listen, Mum,' he instructed her. 'We're going down these stairs, across the landing and then down the servant's staircase at the back. When we get to the bottom, you'll have to walk out through the entrance hall and the main door of the building. No one will take any notice of you. It's pandemonium down there. When you get outside, turn left and walk down Boulevard Descartes to the first street on the right. It's called Rue Puget. Cross over and go down it. Walk slowly and I'll catch you up. Understand?'

His mother nodded.

'And by the way,' Jacob added, 'if you need it, my code name's Nuisance.'

'Nuisance by name, nuisance by nature,' his mother whispered and she briefly kissed him on the cheek. The scab on her lips was rough, like a scaly, dried wart.

'No time to lose, Mum . . .'

They stepped over the dead *SD* guard and into the radio office. In passing it, Jacob picked up the half-empty cup of coffee and poured it into the ventilation holes on the top of the radio casing. There was a brief flash of sparks as the valves inside short-circuited and burned out.

On the landing Jacob was glad to hear the sounds of confusion below had not diminished. He bundled his mother through the door on to the back stairs and in less than two minutes they were on the ground floor.

'Are you ready?' Jacob whispered.

'As I'll ever be,' his mother replied.

Jacob opened the door a few centimetres. A Gestapo officer, a pistol in his hand, was chivvying a number of soldiers carrying boxes.

'Wait!' Jacob hissed. He picked up one of the storage boxes beside the door, emptied the contents on to the stairs and gave it to his mother. 'Remember, once out-side, turn left.'

He opened the door wide. His mother, the empty box clutched to her chest, walked into the entrance hall. Jacob let the door swing shut and headed for the coal cellar.

Jacob briefly poked his head up through the coal hole. Some metres away lay the dead Gestapo officer. At the far end of the alley, on the Boulevard Descartes, a chain of soldiers was loading boxes into a lorry. Certain he was not being observed and kicking against the side of the coal chute, Jacob hoisted himself up. Ammunition was still exploding in the distance, the occasional bullet hitting the building above him and whining off into the sky.

As he walked towards the boulevard, Jacob paused to pick up the Luger, thrusting it down in his waistband and covering it with his shirt.

From the entrance to the alley, he set off at a steady pace. He wanted to run but to have done so would have been foolish, drawing attention to himself and, no doubt, gunfire as well. Yet the Germans were too busy to pay a mere child any attention. Those not occupied loading the lorry were tending the wounded, sweeping the broken glass into the gutter, trying to free the driver from the staff car or securing the immediate area with soldiers taking up defensive positions.

With every step, Jacob expected to be challenged but, as he drew nearer and nearer to the corner of Rue

Puget, so he grew more and more elated. He had pulled it off.

Reaching the balustrade, Jacob turned the corner. On the ground lay the box his mother had been carrying. Fifty metres further along the pavement, she was limping badly, holding on to the wall of a house to steady herself.

Breaking into a run, Jacob came up to her. Her face was ghostly pale, her blackened eye weeping down her cheek. The scab on her lip had split and there was fresh blood smeared across her chin.

'Keep going, Mum,' Jacob encouraged her. 'Just another little bit.'

Thinking on the move, Jacob decided the best thing he could do was to get her to Pierre's café and let the Resistance take over.

'*Halt!*'

Jacob felt as if he had been stabbed in the back. His spine seemed to contract.

'*Bleibt stehen!*'

'*Halt!*'

'*Hände hoch! Hände hoch!*'

Slowly Jacob turned round. Standing across Rue Puget were three German soldiers. Two had their rifles levelled. The other held a sub-machine gun.

Jacob reached inside his shirt. His fingers closed on the butt of the Luger. His thumb eased the safety catch off.

'*Hoch! Hoch!*'

With his left hand, Jacob gave his mother the hardest push he could. She staggered sideways into a doorway. He dropped to one knee, gripped his right wrist with his left hand to steady his aim and raised the Luger.

The German with the sub-machine gun raised the barrel. It pointed directly at Jacob.

Jacob squeezed the trigger of the Luger. It clicked. He stared at it. The firing mechanism had jammed. For a split second, time seemed to be held in abeyance. In that brief moment of limbo, he realized he must have damaged the gun when he threw it at the dead Gestapo officer and he cursed himself for his stupidity.

A sudden burst of gunfire reverberated along Rue Puget. The three German soldiers were lifted off their feet and propelled backwards. Jacob looked at his mother. She was crouched in the doorway, huddled up like a child cowering in a corner but trying frantically to undo the clasp on the pistol holster attached to the SD guard's belt she was wearing.

Beyond her, in the middle of the street, stood Mercator and André. A light haze of blue smoke hung in the air in front of the muzzles of their Stens.

Emile appeared, running to Jacob's mother.

Several more German soldiers came running round the corner with Boulevard Descartes. Mercator and André put down a withering hail of covering fire. They ducked back out of sight.

Lifting Jacob's mother into his arms as if she were no heavier than a little girl, Emile disappeared up Rue Puget with her.

Jacob, dropping the useless Luger, sped after them as fast as he could.

8

In his room at La Tour, Jacob sat on a chair by the bed. His mother lay curled up under a blanket, asleep. Her face had been washed by Madame Aubry and her hands bandaged. All her other wounds and some burn marks on her arms were now a deep mauve colour with a dabbing of gentian violet.

'Jacob . . .'

He turned. Mercator was standing on the stairs, beckoning to him. On tiptoe, Jacob left his mother to join Mercator outside. The sun had dipped behind the trees, the sky patterned with pink herringbone clouds promising a fine night and another hot day in the morning.

'How is she, son?'

'Sleeping,' Jacob said.

'I should be downright furious with you,' Mercator said.

'Yes,' Jacob agreed meekly. 'I know.'

'As it is,' Mercator went on, 'I'm not. I couldn't be. Without you, this operation would have been delayed until Angelique's sister was well enough to help her, and it was imperative that we destroy the fuel dump as soon as possible, in as spectacular a fashion as possible.' He took out his pipe and started to fill it from his tobacco pouch. 'I don't think we could have put on a better show, do you?'

'No,' Jacob agreed.

Mercator tamped down the tobacco in the pipe bowl, struck a match against the wall of the tower and lit up.

'There's more to war than fighting and killing,' he went on. 'You have to also give hope to those who are oppressed. The French are having a very hard time of it. Food's getting scarce in the towns and cities. Their lives are becoming a daily grind under the heel of the Nazi jackboot. Half the country – the southern half, Vichy France, it's called – has sided with Germany. Not to mention the collaborators. The rest are ashamed at this treachery. To see the dump go up boosts their morale. Then there was your little escapade . . .'

'I'm sorry,' Jacob said contritely.

'There's no need for that!' Mercator exclaimed. 'The word's gone round the town – and you can bet your boots it's spreading like wildfire across the region – that the Gestapo have been made to look right fools by an English schoolboy. You can imagine what that will do for morale.'

He puffed on his pipe. The swallow nesting there dived into the eaves above their heads. Its arrival was greeted by a series of tiny, high-pitched cheeps.

'Do you remember what I said a few days ago?' Mercator asked. 'I said there was a fine line between stupidity and courage.'

'Was it only a few days ago?' Jacob mused. It seemed

to him, in retrospect, that he had been in occupied France for weeks.

Mercator laughed. 'Yes, only a couple of days.' He shook his pipe to dislodge a block of spittle from the stem. 'I still think that, about bravery and idiocy. One has to put aside reason to face danger. If you stopped to weigh up the odds, you'd pack your bag and go home.' He sucked on his pipe again. It had gone out. 'What you did, though, wasn't stupid. It was incredibly brave. You could have been killed.'

'I almost was,' Jacob interrupted. 'If it hadn't been for you and André . . .'

'Glad to have been of service,' Mercator replied, 'but that's our job here. It's not yours.'

'I had to do it. She's my mother,' Jacob said bluntly.

'Indeed she is,' Mercator responded. 'And she is a very brave woman. I can see where you get it from.' He knocked his pipe out on the wall, put it back in his pocket and continued, 'Our firework display this afternoon has, not surprisingly, kicked over the Nazi beehive. The Germans have rounded up every male in the town between the age of twelve – thanks to you! – and forty for questioning. Search patrols are fanning out through the surrounding villages. It's only a matter of time before they reach here. We must be prepared.'

The door of La Tour opened. Jacob's mother came out, walking with measured steps in the soft, fleece-lined slippers Madame Aubry had lent her.

Jacob went to his mother's side and took her hand, careful not to squeeze her fingers.

'I have something I must tell you,' she said to Mercator, her words still slurred but now, it seemed to

Jacob, firmer, more assured, more like his mother's voice.

'Later,' Mercator said, 'when you're rested.'

'It can't wait,' she insisted. 'You've been compromised. The whole group has. There's a traitor among us. I was interrogated by a Gestapo *Sturmbannführer*. He bragged as much to me. He didn't give me the traitor's name, of course, but I've deduced it from the facts he let slip.'

'Are you certain?'

'Yes.'

She glanced down the orchard. At the far end, Pierre and Guillaume were keeping watch on the village.

'So?' Mercator asked.

'It's Guillaume.'

Mercator looked hard at Jacob's mother for a moment then he sauntered off down the orchard, the setting sun on his back.

'Mum,' Jacob said, 'you should come inside and rest. It's going to be a long night.'

As he helped his mother to sit down at the table in the tower there came, from the distance, the sharp report of a single pistol shot.

Five minutes later Pierre burst into the tower, Mercator hard on his heels.

'There's a *Schützenpanzerwagen* in the village. Plus a lorry-load of *SS* storm troopers. Three more of ordinary soldiers. Out of the blue. Tipped off, no doubt. But,' Mercator added ominously, 'it won't happen again. We're leaving now.'

Jacob headed smartly for the stairs.

'Where're you off to, Nuisance?'

'Get my satchel,' Jacob said.

'No time for that. Out . . .'

Madame Aubry met them by her cottage.

'I will – how do you put it? – spring-clean La Tour,' she said to Mercator. 'They will not know you were here.'

'*Merci beaucoup, madame*,' Mercator replied and, taking her hand, he kissed it as if she were a courtly lady. 'Take care of yourself. If you need help . . .'

'I shall bluff it out. I am just a foolish old French woman.'

'Thank you, Madame . . .' Jacob began.

She briefly touched his cheek and said, 'Always be a nuisance like you have been in France. Now, no more words! Go! Go!'

Jacob, his mother, Mercator and Pierre headed along the path that went towards the river and the road but, halfway down it Pierre, who was in the lead, stopped. They all dropped to a crouch. Through the trees ahead, Jacob could just discern the outline of a man. Mercator drew them together in a huddle.

'Jacob,' he whispered urgently, 'you and your mother go with Pierre. He'll take you to the landing site. I'll draw this lot off.'

'Where shall we meet you?' Jacob hissed.

'Just you go, Jacob,' Mercator replied. 'Get your mother to safety. Don't worry. I'll make it through.'

He murmured a few words to Pierre and slipped away through the grass towards the vineyard.

'*Allez!*' Pierre said softly.

They struck off through a small copse and into a field of maize, the stalks tall enough to give them cover, the cobs swelling but still some weeks off ripe. Jacob's mother found the going hard but did not complain. At the other side of the field they came upon a narrow lane. Just as they were about to take to it, there came a sustained burst of gunfire from the direction of Belmont. It ceased as suddenly as it started. Pierre genuflected briefly, making the sign of the cross over his chest.

It was then that Jacob felt a painful emptiness swelling within him. It was a mixture of sadness and disappointment and unfulfilled longing. He knew he would never see Mercator again, but he wanted to think that, somewhere in the world he was still alive, still smoking his pipe and enjoying a glass of wine. Now, in his mind, all he saw was the vague figure of a man lying in a vineyard, crumpled up like a discarded doll, his blood seeping into the dry summer earth.

In the late dusk, they arrived at an isolated farm. There were no lights on but Pierre knocked quietly on the door.

A muted voice enquired after their identity through the timbers of the door.

'*C'est Lapin*,' Pierre replied quietly.

A key turned in a lock and the door opened upon a room in pitch darkness. They entered it, the door closed, the key turning once again. Another door then opened to admit an old stooped man carrying a lantern, the flame barely showing. By its light, Jacob could see that the door had been opened by a second man with only one arm, his left eye covered by a patch, the cheek beneath it badly scarred.

Behind the stooped man came a diminutive elderly woman with a tray bearing five glasses and a bottle of brandy. The man ushered Jacob's mother to a chair. Making no distinction for Jacob being a boy, the woman poured out five measures of brandy and handed the glasses round. Jacob sniffed at the liquid. It was pungent and made his nose tickle. When he sipped it, it scoured his throat like acid. The one-armed man grinned toothlessly as Jacob grimaced and winked at him, miming he take another sip.

Throughout all this, no one spoke until, at last, Pierre broke the silence.

''E,' Pierre nodded in the direction of the stooped man, "as a . . .' He searched for the words in English.

'A pony and trap,' Jacob's mother said for him. 'He is Fox and his wife is Vixen. The one-armed man is Cub.'

'*Vous êtes Valerian*,' the old man suddenly declared in a scratchy voice.

'Ah!' his wife exclaimed, throwing her hands in the air as if in supplication and kissing Jacob's mother on both cheeks.

Warmed by the brandy, Jacob went with Pierre to a stable across a field from the house. The night sky was now clear, with only intermittent scattered cumulus clouds. The air had a chilly edge to it. The moon had not yet risen.

'What time is it?' he asked.

Pierre produced an enamel-faced pocket watch from his jacket and angled it to catch the starlight. 'More than eleven,' he said. 'We must go quick.'

'How far do we still have to go?'

'*Dix kilometres*. For you, six mile. But the way,' his hand made undulating movements in mid-air, 'it is not good.'

Inside the stable a lantern burned on a very low wick. By its light Jacob could just make out a two-wheeled dog cart with a pony already harnessed to it, standing patiently tethered to an iron ring in the wall and eating hay from an iron basket. As Jacob led the pony towards the farmhouse he noticed that, behind the wheels, there had been tied two bundles of twigs bound by wire. They made a swishing sound on the ground. It was not until he reached the farmhouse that he realized the purpose of the bundles. They erased any sign of the wheel tracks in the dust.

His mother safely seated on one side of the dog cart and covered with a blanket, Jacob and Pierre sat on the other. Pierre took the reins and they set off at a smart trot. For fifteen minutes they followed a maze of lanes, not one junction in which bore a signpost. Finally they reached a steep-sided, wooded valley. The track they were following deteriorated into two grooves of loose stones. The pony made very slow progress down the valley. When the track doubled back on itself, negotiating the steep hairpin bend necessitated Jacob taking the reins while Pierre got out and walked the pony round the obstacle.

At the bottom of the valley was a wide stream running over a rocky bed. Here, Jacob led the pony across, the water up to his knees, the stones loose and slippery. On the other bank, the pony struggled to pull the dog cart up the slope but Pierre seemed to have a way with the animal, whispering and humming to it until it made a final effort and the wheels cleared the water.

The track up the other side of the valley was not as precipitous as the one they had come down. Jacob sat next to his mother who was reaching the limits of her strength. She drifted in and out of a doze, her head lolling then, as if she was suddenly being jerked awake, coming upright again.

'It's all right, Mum,' Jacob encouraged her. 'It's not far now.' He looked across at Pierre. 'Are we going to the field where I landed?'

'No,' Pierre answered, 'not that place.' He shrugged. 'Guillaume – maybe he tell that place to the Germans.'

Out of the valley, the countryside levelled off into fields, woods and rough heath land. Pierre followed a lane so narrow that at times the bushes on either side snatched at the dog cart. At about one o'clock they halted by a pond.

'*Restez ici,*' Pierre ordered. 'I come back ten minute.'

Jacob let the pony drink at the water's edge. He kept a tight grip on the reins and did not let the creature drink its fill. That, he knew, would slow it down. A short while later, Pierre returned. 'Good!' was all he said.

They moved off, passed through a thick belt of trees and came out on to a flat meadow. Pierre reined the pony in close to the trees and tethered it to a stout sapling. Cupping his hands together, he blew through his thumbs to make a short, owlish hoot. It was answered almost immediately. Two shadowy figures detached themselves from the trees a hundred metres away and ran towards the dog cart.

As they drew close, one of them said in a low voice, '*Bonsoir, Nuisance.*' It was André. At his side was Emile.

'Do we have to wait long?' Jacob asked André.

In reply, André put his hand to his ear. '*Écoutez!*'

Jacob listened. Through the stillness of the night he

could just discern what might have been a faint droning.

As the three men ran off to position themselves with their torches to guide the Lysander down, Jacob helped his mother out of the dog cart.

'Jacky,' she said quietly, 'if there's going to be trouble, it'll happen after the Lysander has landed. Be alert.'

The sound of the Lysander's engine increased in volume. Jacob strained his eyes against the night sky but he could not make out the aircraft's location. Not until it touched down did he manage to see it.

Very quickly, the aircraft taxied towards the dog cart, turning side-on to it. The pony stamped its hoof with alarm then settled down. The engine pitch dropped considerably but the pilot did not switch it off nor, as had happened when Jacob had arrived in France, did he get out of the cockpit. André came running up with Emile. Pierre remained out in the field.

Sliding the canopy open, Emile dropped into the rear compartment to reappear with two canvas bags. He let them fall to the ground and André threw them into the dog cart. Four more bags followed before Emile got out of the Lysander.

Without speaking, they put their arms around Jacob's mother and carried her to the aircraft, pushing her up the steps into the rear compartment. She had difficulty getting her legs over the rim of the canopy and fell rather than lowered herself into the aircraft. Jacob stood behind them waiting his turn.

A ragged line of what looked like sparks flickered in the trees. It was immediately followed by the staccato chatter of a heavy machine gun. The earth twenty metres behind the Lysander erupted as if it were boiling.

Out in the field, Pierre returned fire with his Sten.

Emile grabbed Jacob round the waist, lifting him up bodily. At the same time, André thrust something hard and cold into Jacob's hand.

'*Un souvenir de la guerre,*' André shouted over the cacophony of gunfire. Without looking at it, Jacob tossed the item into the aircraft.

The next Jacob knew was that he was in the Lysander, on the floor of the rear compartment and the aircraft was moving, turning, accelerating. The engine was screaming, the aircraft bucking wildly as it hurtled across the field. Jacob pulled himself up. The slipstream was tearing into the compartment, tugging at his hair, his clothes.

Using all the strength he could muster, Jacob pulled the canopy over. Just as it clicked shut, there was a loud thud. A hole the size of his thumb appeared in the first panel of perspex, not fifty centimetres from the fuel tank.

Then all of a sudden, the bucking stopped. The Lysander climbed sharply, banked and began its steady ascent to its cruising altitude.

Finding two thick army blankets on the floor of the compartment, Jacob unfolded them and, sitting next to his mother on the narrow seat, wrapped her in one of them. As he shook the other blanket out to cover himself, something heavy fell from it to clatter on the compartment floor. He looked down. By the glimmer of the starlight he saw, lying against the bulkhead, the dead Gestapo officer's Luger which he had dropped in Rue Puget that afternoon.

'Exeter were hit hard last night,' the postman declared as he swung his leg over the saddle, dismounted from his bicycle and leaned it against the farmyard gatepost. 'They Luftwaffe bombers almost hit the cathederel they did.' He thumbed through the letters. 'Four today, Mrs Shawcross. None,' he glanced at Jacob, 'from far-off India, I'm afraid.'

Jacob turned, picked up the shovel and started off towards the barn. He had not received a letter from his father since the one that had been delivered the day before his departure for France. The next, he reasoned, had to arrive any day now.

'But,' the postman went on, his voice louder, 'there is a parcel here for . . .' He smoothed the label out. '. . . one Mister J. Adams. Now I wonder who that can be? You know a Mister J. Adams, Mrs Shawcross?'

'Well, I think I just might,' Jacob's grandmother replied.

Jacob leaned the shovel against the milk churn platform.

'No stamps on it, though,' the postman continued, lifting a large package out of the wicker basket in front of the handlebars of his bicycle. 'It's one of they O.H.M.S. letters – On His Majesty's Service. Government mail. Official, that.'

He handed it to Jacob. It was heavy and tied around several times with thick hessian twine.

'Well,' his grandmother enquired, 'aren't you going to open it?'

In the kitchen, Jacob placed the parcel carefully on the table, removed one of his grandfather's butcher's knives from a drawer in the dresser and slit the string.

The wrapping fell aside to reveal two packages, one oblong and the other flat and square. The twine around them was tied in a bow. Jacob tore the flat one open. Inside it was his satchel. The oblong package contained a wooden box fastened with small brass catches. Easing these apart, Jacob lifted the lid. Inside, cosseted in a bed of straw was a bottle of wine. The label, printed in an ornate typeface, read: *Huet Vouvray 'Le Haut Lieu' Moelleux*. Beneath it was printed the date of bottling – 1921.

Carefully tilting the bottle in its box, Jacob said quietly, 'He made it through.'

Tucked into the flap of the satchel was a letter. Jacob removed it and ran outside, climbing up to the top of the farmyard wall. Once seated there, he unfolded it.

Dear Nuisance, he read, *I am sure you will need this when school starts again in September. What a tale it could tell, if only it could speak, eh? And what a story you could, too. But I'm sure you've been told not to blab, at least until this war is over, and I know you won't. Alas! all your other belongings – hip flask, penknife – were taken when the SS reached the tower. The bottle, you will note, is your favourite tipple. Wine, however, does not travel well by air. The altitude affects it. Consequently, I asked Wing Commander – you know who – to fly back at zero feet. I trust he did. Look after yourself. Your friend and comrade-in-arms, Mercator. Postscript: A, E & P send their regards – Madame A sends her love.*

Folding the letter once more, Jacob put it in his pocket, jumped down from the wall and went into the farmhouse kitchen. The radio was on, playing dance music. His grandmother was standing at the table kneading a lump of dough, pushing it out with her knuckles, pulling it back into a ball, turning it over, slapping it down on the table top and starting the motion again. Sitting opposite her, folding laundry into a basket, was his mother. Her ear was bandaged, the bruising around her eye was already fading and three of her fingers were encased in plaster of Paris. She was humming along with the music.

'Gran,' Jacob asked, removing the bottle of Vouvray from its box, 'please can I have the corkscrew?'

Chapter 5 is loosely based upon the true story of two teenage French girls (aged 14 and 16) who, using carborundum paste provided by the SOE, caused every single German tank transporter lorry in an entire Panzer division to break down on 7 June 1944, thus preventing it from taking part in the attack on Allied troops in Normandy for over a week. This considerably aided the Allied advance into France after the D-Day invasion of the day before.

Glossary

altimeter	a cockpit flight instrument that gives the aircraft's current height above sea level
artificial horizon	a cockpit flight instrument that tells the pilot how he is flying in relation to the horizon – in other words, in level flight or not
Ausweis	a pass or identity document
A votre santé	the French equivalent of 'Cheers!': literally, 'to your health'
Bleibt stehen!	Stand still!
un boulevard	a wide street, often lined by trees
C'est de l'eau, très froide	It's water, very cold
Französisches Blag!	French brat!
Gestapo	the common name for the Nazi *Geheime Staatspolizei*, the state secret police

Halifax	the Handley Page Halifax, a heavy bomber named after the city in Yorkshire
Hände hoch!	Hands up!
Hau ab!	Get lost
Il est quatre heures moins cinq	It's five to four
Il fait chaud	It's hot
Ils sont des animaux	They are animals
l'ivrogne	drunkard
Les Boches	The Boche – a derogatory term for the Germans
Il est temps de partir, m'sieur	Time to go, sir
M Busson et Fils – Marchands de Mais	Mr Busson & Son – Corn Merchants
La Marseillaise	the French national anthem
Mon oncle est bu	My uncle is drunk
Ne bougez pas!	Don't move!
perspex	a transparent plastic used in aircraft windows in place of glass
un pissoir	an open-air gent's lavatory
Pourquoi tu n'es pas à l'école, cet après-midi	Why aren't you at school this afternoon?
Qu'est-que vous?	What are you about?

Schützenpanzerwagen	a half-track German armoured personnel carrier with a light machine gun mounted on it
SD	the initials of the *Sicherheitsdienst*, the intelligence service of the *SS* (see below). Its role was to gather information in conjunction with the Gestapo in Nazi-occupied countries
SS-Gruppenführer	a major-general in the *Schutzstaffel* (or *SS*), the elite German security police
Sten	a British Sten gun, an easily used and assembled machine carbine, a favourite of both the SOE and French Resistance fighters
Sturmbannführer	the equivalent rank in the Gestapo to a Major in the British army
Un souvenir de la guerre	A souvenir of the war
Une glace, Jacob? Un jus d'orange, peut-être?	An ice cream, Jacob? An orange juice, perhaps?
Was ist es, Hans?	What's up, Hans?
Was zum Teufel machst du da?	What the hell do you think you're doing?
Wo willst du denn hin?	Where do you think you're going?

Dangerous magic — ancient enemies

Doctor Illuminatus

MARTIN BOOTH

Sebastian is the alchemist's son,
pursuing his father's enemies
through the centuries.

Caught in a web of magic and
cunning, Pip and Tim's only hope
of escape is to join the desperate battle
against unimaginable evil.

A fantastical tale of sorcery and betrayal

Sebastian's battle against the dark side of
alchemy continues in

Soul Stealer

MARTIN BOOTH

the second book about the alchemist's son.

This time the danger comes from a new
and unexpected source. Someone possesses
Gerbert d'Aurrillac's book of spells – and
intends to use it to deadly effect.

If someone steals your bicycle, you
buy another.

But what if they steal your soul . . .?

To be published spring 2004